Pankaj's Short Stories

Pankaj Modak

Published by PSS Publisher, 2024.

This is a work of fiction. Similarities to real people, places, or events are entirely coincidental.

PANKAJ'S SHORT STORIES

First edition. November 7, 2024.

Copyright © 2024 Pankaj Modak.

ISBN: 979-8227052933

Written by Pankaj Modak.

Pankaj's Short Stories

Pankaj Modak

Draft2Digital's

Pankaj's Short Stories

About The Author

My name is Pankaj Modak. I am a Short story writer. I was born in Chandaha, a village in India, which is located in the state of Jharkhand. My father is Shankar Modak and my mother is Lalita Devi. I have two elder brothers and an elder sister.

Thoughts Of Author

Keep working hard and trying. In the end two

things will happen - you will succeed or you will perish. But there will be a satisfaction in my mind that I had tried.

Enjoy life, you will not get life again.

Death is fun only when death comes automatically.

Money is useful only as long as you are alive.

Violence to save one's own life or the life of another is not bad.

Most crimes happen late at night.

Only God (nature) has the right to give death penalty.

By failing in board exams, you do not fail in life.

By doing bad deeds, good flowers do not bloom in your life.

By not helping, the chances of getting help decrease.

The biggest dream should be to 'Life enjoyer'. So that later one does not regret that he could not enjoy life.

Effect Of Camphor - Shankar's father Vijay was working in B.C.C.L. When Shankar was 12 years old, Vijay used to come home drunk and beat up Shankar's mother Sumu Devi. Shankar used to get sad seeing this. Shankar had a friend named Narayan. They were in the same class and studied together. They passed 10th standard. At that time, there was almost no possibility of a vehicle in the village. Both of them got enrolled in a college in the city. If they had any work to do in the college, they had to walk 15 kilometers to reach there. Shankar had five sisters, who were older than him. At that time, there was no college near the village. There was a bullock cart facility in the village, but it did not go that far. They passed the 12th standard examination. Now both of them got enrolled for BA in a university in Patna. Shankar's father used to go to work only occasionally. The rest of the days he used to remain drunk. Therefore, he used to come home with a very low salary. It was difficult to run the household. Looking at the financial condition of the house, he had to leave his studies. He had studied almost till B.A. Part 2. Shankar ji was now roaming around in search of a job. One day Shankar ji came to know that a broker was recruiting constables. Shankar ji went to the broker. The broker said- You will have to pay 50 thousand for recruitment. But his father knew that this broker will cheat him. Therefore Vijay ji did not give money to Shankar ji. Shankar ji now started selling coal. Bringing coal from the mine on a bicycle in the scorching sun and then selling it. It was a very difficult job. At the age of 21, Shankar ji got married to a girl named Lalita. Now Shankar ji left the coal business and started selling fish. One day some fishermen stole fish from the pond of Babu village. That day some people were standing on the road to catch a fish seller. At that time Shankar ji was going that way. People stopped him. People started abusing and scolding him. Shankar ji had not done anything. Still he was listening to everything. After that he left the job of selling fish and opened a hardware shop with the money he had saved. He used to go to fairs sometimes and sell chickpeas. His wife gave birth to their first child. But due to illness that child could not survive and he died. Similarly the second child also could not survive due to illness. After that they had a daughter. After that three more sons were born. One day Shankar ji got dysentery. He had heard from some elders that dysentery is cured by consuming camphor. Shankar ji took his bicycle and left for a shop to buy camphor. He reached the shop. He bought a camphor and started towards home. He consumed the camphor after reaching home. After some time, he started jumping. Everyone and his family members were watching everything. The effect of camphor was so strong that Shankar ji was not able to bear it. The family members got worried about what happened to him. After some time the effect of camphor reduced. Shankar ji became normal. Everyone and family members started asking him - what happened to you? Shankar ji told everything. Then everyone came to know that this was the effect of camphor. Many years passed. With his hard work and struggle, he changed the small shop into a good hardware shop. Where more than 200 products and materials are available. He built a good and big house. Which is standing firmly even after more than 25 years. Where good and cool breezes come.

Refuse - A girl named Salima. She used to go for tuition in the ninth grade. There she fell in love with a boy. Slowly it turned into love. After several days, the boy came to Salima and said- I want to marry you. Salima said- You will have to talk to my parents. The boy flatly refused to talk and said- Let's elope. The girl refused to elope and went towards her home. From the next day onwards, there was no conversation or meeting between them. Slowly, the anger in the boy increased. After a few days, the desire to take revenge arose in the boy. It was before noon. Salima was coming home from the guest house on her scooty. Now her house was at some distance. She was leisurely going towards home on her scooty. That day she was not wearing a helmet. The boy hit the back of the scooty while driving his bike at a high speed. Salima fell some distance away along with the scooty. The girl suffered serious injuries. A lot of blood started flowing from her body. A crowd of people gathered there. After some time her parents came there. They picked up their daughter and started taking her to the hospital in a car. Salima also had serious injuries on her forehead. After some time Salima breathed her last in the car itself and died. Tears started flowing from the eyes of her parents. After some days the police investigated and the boy was caught. But the boy's father proved his son innocent by bribing the lawyers and police officers. After some days, after a large amount of money was transferred to the bank accounts of the corrupt lawyers and officers, the income tax officers arrested them and started questioning them. A few weeks passed. It was night time. The boy was driving his car drunk. He started losing control over the car. The car was going at a very high speed.

There was a bridge ahead. The car collided with the bridge's rails and fell down and he died.

Last Wish - Vijay ji. He was born in a small village in India. He was employed in B.C.C.L. The salary was good, but he used to earn a thousand rupees. He used to go to work only occasionally and used to remain drunk on other days. That is why he used to earn less salary. He was married to a girl named Sumu. He had five daughters and one son. One day Vijay ji went to work as usual. But he did not return home. It was evening. Sumu was feeling nervous. A person came to his house and said that Vijay ji is lying drunk on the bank of Lal Dam. My father went there and brought him back the next day. Sumu explained to him that drinking alcohol is not good for health. But it did not have any effect on Vijay ji. He was fond of planting trees. He had planted many trees. Some people came to Vijay ji and said- Dogs are killing our goats. Vijay ji got excited and said- I will kill the dogs. He made a bow and made many pointed arrows. He started killing dogs. He killed two-three dogs. Some years passed. Vijay ji had become old now. His hair had turned white. Alcohol had weakened his body. Now he did not go to work. He did not have that strength in his body. Now he would lie on the cot most of the time. Vijay ji started telling his family members. I will not be able to survive for many more days. The next day his daughters were called from their parents' house. There was sadness on the faces of all the family members. They called their grandsons. They gave two rupees each in their hands. The villagers also came to his house. Vijay ji was regretting killing the dogs at the last moment. Everyone was standing beside him. At the last moment he expressed his last wish. He said - I want to drink alcohol. Everyone was surprised to hear this. But everyone ignored his words and started feeding him milk. The elder son of Vijay ji's elder daughter was standing there watching everything. His name was Puna. He bought two-three packets of liquor from a small hotel nearby and brought it home. When Vijay ji saw the liquor, a happy face appeared on his face. Puna tore the packet and started pouring it in his mouth. After some time of drinking liquor, he stopped breathing. There was silence there. The whole house was drowned in grief. Everyone started crying bitterly. Vijay ji died and he left this world. (Chapter 4) Two Brothers - Two brothers lived on top of a tree. They had no home. One was ten years old and the other was around eleven years old. Their parents died a few years after their birth. The first brother's name was Megan and the second brother's name was Egan. Their relatives had also left them. These two brothers used to survive by eating the fruits and leaves of the tree. All they had was a few words spoken by their father at the last moment. Their father had said. When you leave this world, go famous. Both of them used to sit on the tree and listen to the people sitting under the tree. Slowly time passed. One day two people were sitting under the tree. Those two people were talking about something. Both the brothers sitting on the tree were listening to those people carefully. Those two people were saying that if there are trees in the world, there is life. This thing got stuck in the minds of those brothers. They got a big task to do something in the world. They started planting trees at various places. Many times people would say to them- son, study at this age, why are you doing this? But they did not back off from planting trees. Now they had only one goal. To spread greenery all over the world. One day some people were cutting trees. Those two brothers informed the police about this. The police caught those tree cutters. Some years passed. Now both of them grew up. The two brothers never considered their work to be small. Both of them kept doing their work. There was a desert at a distance of a few kilometers. Where not even a single tree was present. Both of them decided to make the desert green. Both of them got busy in planting, watering and growing trees in the desert. People started calling those two brothers mad. But those brothers kept busy in their work. About ten years passed. Now the desert had become green. There were many trees there. Where hot winds used to blow. Today cold winds were blowing there. Now it was not a desert but a green forest. Those people who used to call them mad. Today they were making them famous. They were being praised everywhere. The government gave them national level awards. Many invitations started coming for those two brothers from abroad as well. After many years, those two brothers made foreign deserts green as well. They also received many international level awards. The record of planting the maximum number of trees in the whole world was registered in the name of those two brothers. Those two brothers became famous all over the world due to their work. Both of them became almost a hundred years old. Both of them filled a form. In which after the death of both of them, the organs present in their bodies should be given to someone else. Slowly time passed. After a few days, their breathing stopped and they died. Even after death, there was a kind of smile on the faces of those two brothers.

To Star Side - A child was born at night. At that

time thousands of stars were twinkling in the sky. The whole world was shining with the light of thousands of stars. The parents named their child Taru. Taru started growing up slowly. He would often look at the stars while sleeping at night. He would say to his father, Papa, one day I will go to the stars. The father would say- yes son. He passed the twelfth standard at the age of eighteen. He was very interested in geography. Slowly time passed. Taru did his PhD in Geography at the age of twenty-six. He had now become Dr. Taru. He got a job in a space organization. Taru, along with his fellow space workers, started building a rocket that could go to the stars. Years passed by. They all continued with their work. After about ten years, an advanced rocket was built. Taru said- I want to go to the stars by rocket. But everyone refused and said that going there or for any human being can be life threatening. Because stars are extremely hot. There is neither air nor water in them. Everyone decided to send a robot wearing a space suit on the rocket. Taru had worked very hard in making that rocket. Therefore, everyone named that rocket Taru-1. The satellite was to be launched from that rocket. The next day. It was morning time. Sunlight was spread all around. Many people came to see the rocket test. Taru sat in the rocket wearing a space suit and stood still like a robot. Everyone thought that it was a robot. The rocket was launched. The rocket took off. Smoke went everywhere. The rocket started moving towards space, tearing through the sky. After a few days, the workers working in the space agency came to know that Taru was sitting in the rocket instead of a robot. This news reached his parents. His parents started crying a lot. A strong stream of tears flowed from their eyes. Now nothing can be done. Now the rocket had gone quite far. The rocket kept moving towards the star. Days kept passing. After about six months, the rocket had now reached near the star. The heat was very intense. The ration and water present in the rocket had finished. The satellite was launched. The satellite started revolving around the star. Everyone saw the land of the star through the camera present in the satellite. Which was very hot and only hot lava was visible. Taru started moving towards the star. He was unable to bear the bright light of the star. His whole body was drenched in sweat due to heat. As he kept moving towards the stars, his body started melting. Taru's dream of going to the stars was about to be fulfilled. Despite so much pain and burning, there was a strange satisfaction and a strange smile on Taru's face. After some time, Taru merged into the stars. The eyes of the people of the whole world became moist and that space scientist left this world.

Telu - An eighteen year old youth named Telu. He would just eat and lie down on the bed. He would not do any work inside or outside the house. He would just rest. His mother used to do household chores. His father was employed in a government office. His parents would often scold Telu to do some work, otherwise how would they manage their life. But Telu would not pay heed to their words. Slowly time passed. One day Telu's father fell ill. His mother and father would always remain worried and sad thinking about their son. Due to being sad, his father's health was gradually deteriorating. His father would no longer go to office. Now he would lie on cots due to illness. Now the savings were slowly getting exhausted. A lot of money had been spent on his father's treatment. But due to sadness and worry, there was no improvement in his health. Like this a few years passed. Now they had only a few rupees left. It was morning time. Light cold winds were blowing. When Telu's mother came to see her husband, her husband had stopped breathing. Telu's mother started crying bitterly. After some time, the people of the village gathered there. Telu was standing there sadly looking at his father. After some time, his father's body was cremated. After a few days, Telu's mother mortgaged the house to a businessman named Malan and got some money. A feast was started with that money. Many types of dishes and food items were prepared. Many people ate and left. The next day, Telu was lying on the cot in the same way. His mother remained immersed in the grief of her husband. Due to which her body started becoming weak. Now she would not even eat food on time. After a few days, the mother also died. The mother's body was cremated. Telu did not organize any kind of feast. After a few days, Malan Seth took over that house. Now Telu had neither parents nor home. He had one thing. That was laziness. Telu now started going towards the forest. All the people of the village were calling him lazy. Due to not working, Telu's stomach had bloated due to obesity. He sat under a tree. Due to laziness, Telu had lost the desire to work. Telu had now become a victim of obesity. Now Telu was regretting. But now it was too late. Tears started falling from his eyes and touched the ground.

The Old Woman - Aman named Lameet. One day he returned home after work in the evening. Lameet had a wife named Talisha. They were married a few years ago. But they had no children. As soon as Lameet came home, an argument started between Lameet and his wife on some issue. This argument gradually turned into a fight. Lameet left the house and started walking towards the forest. Talisha stood at the door and kept staring at her husband. It was night at that time. Stars were twinkling in the sky. The path was somewhat visible in the moonlight. Lameet was walking towards the forest. He heard someone crying. He stopped there. He started looking here and there. He saw an old woman. She was sitting on the ground. She was crying. A lantern was kept on the ground. Lamit went to that old woman and said, Grandma, why are you crying here? The old woman said- Son, I live in a hut, which is built on that small hill over there. Every night the bandits used to come there. Every night I used to leave my house in the evening and after reaching here I used to cry. The bandits used to eat all the food cooked in the house. I cannot do anything. They have a lot of guns and bombs. Lameet thought for some time in his mind and said- Grandma, I will do something such that those bandits will not come to your house again. A happiness appeared on the face of the old woman. Lamit and that old woman came to their hut in the morning. The old woman cooked many types of dishes and fed Lamit. Lamit got busy in the work of planning to drive away the bandits. It was about to be evening. The old woman said goodbye to

Lameet and went towards the forest with a lantern. Lameet climbed up a tall dense tree. After some time the sun set. It became night. The robbers arrived there. As per the plan, Lameet made a huge scary shadow with some things. Lameet started making loud scary sounds. Out of fear, the robbers' hearts started beating loudly, sweat started coming out of their foreheads. Without delaying, the robbers ran away from there. Lameet's plan was successful. After some time, it was morning. The old woman came there. She saw. Lameet was lying on a cot inside the hut. The old woman was happy to see this. The old woman woke up Lameet. Lameet got up. Lameet washed his face and told the old woman about the incident of the night in detail. The old woman happily gave him some gold ornaments. The old woman had saved those gold ornaments from the robbers and buried them under the ground of the hut. After some time, the old woman cooked food. Today too, the food was very tasty. Lameet ate to his heart's content. Lameet said goodbye to the old woman and started walking towards his home with a happy heart.

Sammohan - A boy named Sammohan. His father used to work as a junk dealer. His mother used to work as a housemaid. Sammohan was very interested in books since childhood. He used to spend most of his time reading books. He liked reading robotic books a lot. He was around sixteen years old. The three of them used to live in an old hut. There was a dense forest at a distance of nine hundred meters from their hut. Sammohan had studied only till the eighth grade. One day Sammohan was reading books. An idea came to his mind that why not make a robot. Sammohan got involved in the work of making a robot. He got many kinds of necessary things from the junk lying in the house. He kept on working on making the robot. Time passed slowly. About seven years passed. The robot was ready. The robot was working well. It was night time. The sky was covered with dark clouds. The place where Sammohan was working was covered with sacks. Sammohan had prepared a place to work with the help of sacks. That night Sammohan was feeling very tired. So he slept there. Some short-circuit started in the robot. But Sammohan went into a deep sleep due to fatigue. He could not pay attention to the robot. Due to the short-circuit, the robot lost its temper. The robot moved towards Sammohan to kill him. The robot started strangling Sammohan with its hands. After some time, Sammohan stopped breathing due to suffocation. The robot left from there and walked slowly towards the dense forest. After a few hours, it was morning. When the parents left the hut and went to the place of work, Sammohan was lying there lifeless. The parents started crying a lot after seeing Sammohan. A stream of tears started flowing from their eyes. After some time, a group of ten people picked up Sammohan and started taking him to the forest to bury him. It was afternoon. After some time, they reached the forest. The corpses of many animals were seen lying on the ground. It seemed as if they had been killed a while ago. Seeing this, everyone started trembling. Before people could escape from there, a robot came and started killing people one by one. Some people ran away from there. The corpses of some people remained lying there. Now the battery of the robot also ran out. The robot also fell there lifeless. The people who ran away filed a report in the police station that the robot had killed many people. After some time, police officers reached there. Police officers saw. The corpses of people were lying on the ground. Police officers put the corpses of the villagers in the vehicle and buried the corpses of the animals in the soil. Police officers saw the robot at some distance. They understood that all this was the work of the robot. The officers also put the robot in another vehicle. After some time, the officers reached the village. The officers handed over the corpses to the people present in the village. There was mourning in many families of the village. The family was in grief. The police officers took away the important things present in the robot and smashed it with a hammer and threw it in the junk. The robot lay there broken and broken.

The Old Fort - A fort which was hundreds of years old. That is why people had named that fort Purana Qila (Old Fort). For many days some scary stories had started spreading about that fort. If you go to that fort at night, you will not return, the dead body of the person who goes there at night is found in the morning. A person named Sarim who returned to his country a few days ago after working in America. He also heard all these things. He was not able to believe these things. Sarim decided to go to that old fort to find out the truth. It was morning now. Sarim had his food and went to sleep after half an hour. Sarim was waiting for the night to come. After some time it became night. Sarim woke up from sleep and took an old torch and started walking towards the old fort. The distance of the fort from his house was about one kilometer. There was silence everywhere at night. He kept moving forward. The night had become quite dark. While walking, the torch slipped from Sarim's hand and fell down. The torch got damaged after hitting a stone. Sarim started walking in the dark. He reached near the fort. He saw a torch burning on the upper part of the fort. Some people were sitting in front of the torch. They had sharp axes, swords etc. in their hands. Sarim understood that all of them were dacoits. He had come to know the truth. Sarim started walking towards his house without making any noise while hiding. His heart was beating loudly. He was afraid that some dacoit might come from behind. He was drenched in sweat. After some time he reached near his house. He felt relieved. He thanked God and lay down in his bed. The breakdown of the torch proved to be good for him. One year later. When Sarim was reading his newspaper. It was printed in it that in the old fort, some dacoits died after falling from the fort in a drunken state.

Junior Runner - When Ridam's mother was taking her to the market, her mother died due to firing by people involved in the riots. Ridam was sitting on the road and crying. After some time, police officers came there and took her mother's dead body and handed Ridam over to her father. At that time, Ridam was around 12 years old. After a few days, her father admitted her to an orphanage and married again. Ridam became sad. 10 years later. Ridam was a junior runner. Ridam's performance was getting very bad in the last few competitions. That's why she started feeling more sad for some days. After a few days, a junior running competition was going to be held in the district. Ridam used to work hard day and night for that competition. Now she did not even eat properly. Due to which her body started becoming weak gradually. After a few days, the running competition started. Now all the runners were about to run when Ridam felt dizzy and fell down. Ridam was admitted to the hospital. After a few days, Ridam became healthy. Now she worked hard and ate well from time to time. After 1 year. Again a race competition was organized in the district. This time Ridam came second in the district level race competition. The second time she got third position in the state level race competition. After a few years she participated in the national race competition and again came third. On one hand there was happiness of coming third and on the other hand there was sadness of not coming first. Now she used to do the training given by the coach. Along with that she used to do other exercises also. Like climbing small mountains, running a few kilometers in the morning...etc. Five players including Ridam were selected for the World Olympics. Ridam was leaving everyone behind in the race and was performing very well. The time came when Ridam won gold in the Olympics and came first. She was running waving the flag of her country. Today her father was also present in the stadium and was clapping.

Smart Dog - The wife of a man named Sunet had died due to illness. She had a seven year old son. After some time Suneet got married again. The boy now had a step mother. Everything went well for a few years. But when the step mother had a child, her love for the seven year old boy slowly ended. A dog used to sit under a tree outside the house. The boy used to play with him. Sunet used to go to work in the morning after having breakfast. There used to be daily arguments, scoldings between the step mother and the boy. One day the step mother got fed up of all this and tied the boy with a rope and took him behind her house. There was an old grave lying there. She locked the boy in the grave and buried him in the pit present there. The dog was watching all this at a distance. The dog did not delay and ran to Sunet. Sunet recognized the dog. A lot of tears were visible in the dog's eyes. Sunet started going with the dog. After some time, Sunet reached the place behind the house. The dog told him to dig here. Sunet started digging. After some time, he saw a grave. When he opened the grave, he was shocked. Sunet took his son out of the grave and took him to the hospital. The boy was still breathing. After a few days, the boy recovered. The police officers caught the stepmother. The court sentenced the woman to ten years of imprisonment for this crime.

A Mountain - A beautiful mountain which was in a dense forest. Every year many tourists used to come to climb that mountain. But whoever reached the top of the mountain would not return. Day by day the tourists who climbed it were going missing. A detective named Senan decided that he would find out why so many tourists were going missing. What is the secret of that mountain? It was morning. Dark clouds were engulfing the sky. Senan washed his hands and face and had food and set out alone towards the mountain in a hired car. After a few hours he reached the road which was inside the forest. Senan started going towards the mountain through the rough path of the forest. After some time he reached near that mountain. He started climbing the mountain. He reached a great height of the mountain. He looked up the mountain. On the upper part of the mountain he saw many smiling people who were staring at Senan. Senan did not climb to the top of the mountain but started descending quickly. After some time he reached the bottom. When Senan saw those people, they had one hand behind their back. That means all of them had weapons in their hands behind their back. Their beards, moustaches and nails were quite long. So they were not tourists. They were cannibals. They were killing the tourists coming to the mountain. Senan wrote 'Cannibal' in big letters on the lower part of the mountain with a stone and he started walking towards his home thanking God. After a few years, there was a terrible lightning during the rainy season. Lightning struck that mountain several times one after the other. In this lightning, the cannibal people living on the mountain were killed.

The Old Cave - Two friends whose age was around twenty five years. One was named Segan and the other was named Beman. One day they came to roam in an unknown forest in their jeep. They were walking in the forest. Slow winds were blowing in the forest. That day the sky was covered with dark clouds. They saw two caves. Which looked very old. There were two boards outside both the caves. On one was written - Wealth and on the other was written - Knowledge. In greed of wealth Beman went towards the first cave and Segan went towards the second cave for knowledge. After some time they reached inside the cave. Both of them got whatever was written on the boards. But Beman got wealth and along with it the guards who were protecting the wealth. The wild people used to protect the wealth present in the cave. On the other hand Segan found many books in the second cave. Among those books Segan found a book in which it was written about the second cave. He started reading that book. After reading for a while, he came to know that the people who protect the wealth throw down the people who come to take the wealth from the mountain. The jungle guards started taking Beman towards the mountain. Without delaying, Segan started throwing lots of leaves, husk, straw etc. on the lowest surface of the mountain. After some time, the sun started setting and it became evening. A lot of leaves, husk, straw etc. had accumulated on the lower surface of the mountain. The jungle guards reached the upper surface of the mountain. The guards threw Beman down. Segan was watching all this scene hiding behind a tree below. Beman fell down from the mountain with a thud. Segan without delay reached him. Beman's hands and legs were broken. He started moaning in pain. Seeing Beman alive, the jungle guards started coming down the mountain quickly. Segan somehow picked up Beman from there and made him sit in his jeep.

Segan drove the jeep at high speed straight to the hospital and Beman's life was saved. A few days later the police officers caught the people living in that cave and the gold was confiscated.

Meton - An officer named Meton lived with his family in a village near the forest. Meton has a wife and a four-year-old daughter. One day Meton was looking after the forest in his jeep. Meton saw some smugglers carrying a baby crocodile. Meton pointed his gun at them and said, "Raise your hands." The smugglers raised their hands. Those smugglers were sent to jail. The court sentenced those smugglers to ten years of imprisonment. Those smugglers had killed many animals and sold their body parts. Meton took that baby crocodile to his home and started raising it like his own child. After a few years Meton's wife gave birth to another child. Slowly time passed. Those smugglers were released from jail after completion of ten years. After staying in jail for a long time, they decided to take revenge from that officer. Those smugglers decided to kill the officer's children. Next day when the officer returned home in the evening, he saw many drops of blood on the floor of the house. The crocodile was there. There was blood on its face and its stomach was swollen. The officer thought that the crocodile had betrayed him. It had eaten my children.

The officer got angry and kept attacking the crocodile with an axe. Tears started coming out of the crocodile's eyes. The sound of a child crying was heard from the other room. The officer ran to that room and saw that both the children and his wife were safe. The smugglers were lying injured on the floor of that room. Two-three sharp weapons were also lying there. His wife said - These smugglers had come to kill us. But, the crocodile killed and injured those smugglers and went to the floor of the house and started waiting for you. Meton asked - Why was his stomach swollen? The wife said- the crocodile had swallowed a lot of fruits in the morning. That is why his stomach was bloated. Regret took over the officer's mind. He sat there dejectedly. Tears welled up in his eyes. He was unable to understand anything. He kept crying, wailing and pleading there. But, it was too late now. The crocodile had fallen asleep in the lap of death.

The Pain Of Being Lost - A forest where many animals were living. All the animals were living happily. There was greenery all around. Light winds were blowing. At the same time, sounds of 'Dhai! Dhai!' were heard. Two-three animals fell down. They had been shot. The hunters started firing bullets continuously. The animals started running. Suddenly, the animals started falling on the ground after being shot. The animals were moaning in pain. After some time, their bullets got over. A woman was sitting in their jeep. She had a small child in her hand. The woman had come to the forest with them to see the beautiful natural scenery. But she did not know that this would happen in the forest. As soon as the firing stopped, the animals became furious. The animals started running towards the hunters to attack them. The hunters started climbing into their jeeps in a hurry. In a hurry, the child slipped from the woman's hands and fell on a pile of dry leaves. By then, the jeep started. The woman tried to jump off the jeep. But the hunters caught her. The animals had come very close to the jeep. The jeep started moving. The child's mother was crying bitterly. Tears were dripping from her eyes. The jeep started moving towards the city through the forest. At the same time a hippopotamus was coming out of the pond. The wolf moved towards it to kill the child. The hippopotamus saw this. The hippopotamus came there and saved the child. The hippopotamus and the wolf got into a fight. The hippopotamus got a few injuries. But the hippopotamus defeated the wolf. The hippopotamus started protecting the child from other animals. On the other hand, the hunters were moving towards the city at a fast speed out of fear. The woman was crying. The woman somehow freed her hand from them and jumped off the jeep. Due to which the woman got many scratches on her body and a serious injury on her head. Due to which she fainted right there. There was a deep ditch on the other side of the road. The jeep driver sneezed a few times. Due to which the driver lost the balance of the jeep and the jeep fell into the ditch. The woman was lying unconscious on the road. After a few hours, a forest officer was going on that road in his jeep. He saw the woman. The officer picked up the woman and made her sit in his jeep and took her to the hospital. The hippopotamus waited for its mother at the same place for two days. But she did not come. After more than two days, the hippopotamus took the child to a cave at a little distance. The hippopotamus would feed the child the juice extracted by crushing fruits. It was evening. On the other hand, after a few days, the woman regained consciousness. The woman remembered her child. She started crying again. The sun set completely. It was night. The woman started waiting for the morning. It was morning. The woman sat in a rented car and started alone towards the forest. She got down on the road near the forest. She started going inside the forest. The whole place was shining with sunlight. The chirping of birds was heard. She started searching for her child like mad. But the child was not found. She sat down in despair. It seemed as if the hope of finding the child was now ending. The scorching sun was spread all around. A deer recognized that woman. The deer caught the woman's pallu in its mouth and started pulling the pallu and taking the woman towards the cave. After some time the woman reached near that cave. The child was playing on the grass outside the cave. The hippopotamus was watching the child playing and was feeling happy in his heart. The woman came running. She took her child in her lap and tears of joy flowed from her eyes.

The Cyclone - A person named Sadan was born in a village situated on the seashore. He was poor. He used to take passengers on a boat and take them on a sea trip. His livelihood depended on his work. He lived in an old hut. He had an old radio on which he used to listen to songs and news. Life was going well. He returned home in the evening. At night he was lying on his cot. The news was coming on the radio that the weather may change for thirty days and there is a possibility of storm and cyclone in the sea. Therefore, you should not go near the sea for 30 days. Stay at home. Stay safe. He became sad after hearing this. Due to fatigue, he fell asleep while lying down. It was morning. He took his boat and went towards the sea. After some time he reached the seashore. There was no one around the sea. Slow winds were blowing. The sky was covered with dark clouds. Sadan was sitting sadly on the seashore. After a few hours it was evening. The sun was about to set. Sadan started walking towards his hut dragging his boat. Time passed like this. Two weeks passed. Sadan had run out of money and ration. He started starving. Two days passed. He had become very weak now. Sixteen days had passed. It was morning. Sadan went towards the sea dragging his boat on an empty stomach. Even today there was no one there. He put his boat in the water and lay down in it. He kept staring at the sky for some time. The sky was covered with dark clouds. Strong winds were blowing. Slowly the weather started changing. The waves started rising high. A cyclone developed in the sea. The clouds started thundering. It started raining. Seeing the cyclone Sadan started trembling with fear. He felt that his end was near. He fell unconscious. The waves took Sadan's boat to an island. Sadan's boat was completely broken. Sadan was lying unconscious on the seashore of the island. The cyclone had calmed down. The waves of the sea had become normal. Some local tribals of the island picked Sadan up and took him to their hut. Sadan was woken up. The tribals gave him some fruits to eat. Sadan told the tribals everything. Sadan stayed with them for a few days. Now Sadan felt like going home. But his boat had become useless. Sadan knew this. He went to the seashore where his boat was lying. He was surprised to see the boat. The boat had been completely repaired. He was delighted. He came to know that the tribals had repaired his boat. Sadan thanked the tribals and said goodbye and started walking towards his home. After some time he reached the seashore. There were many travellers present on the shore. Thirty days had passed. He was elated to see the travellers. He thanked the tribals and God in his heart and got busy with his work.

Laghu - A boy named Laghu. He was about thirteen years old. He belonged to a poor family. Laghu was the only child of his parents. One day Laghu was watching TV at his friend's house. Seeing his friend's house sitting at some distance from his house. Both of them were watching TV. A serial called Shaktimaan was running on TV. Both were looking happy. The serial ended after about an hour. Saying goodbye to his friend, Laghu went towards his house. He was strolling. A small mountain was present at some distance from Laghu's house.

He started thinking in his mind. Can I be powerful? Wrong information came to his mind. He reacted at home. He washed his hands, ate and sat on the cot. It was late in the afternoon. Hot winds were blowing. His father had gone to work. After some time it was evening. Now the hot wind outside has changed to cold wind. Laghu started getting up from the bed. Mother asked where are you going son? Laghu said and he went out. Today he lied to his mother for the first time. Laghu started walking towards the mountain. A slow wind was blowing all around. After some time he reacted to the upper part of the mountain. Now the sun was about to set. The sun was seen red in the sky. Laghu jumped down like a shakitan -to spin around. Laghu fell down with a thud. He started moaning in pain. After some time the sun set and his breath stopped.

Mountaineer - A boy named Siriman. He was from a middle poor family. He used to hear many times from his family and friends that Shiva himself resides on the top top of Mount Kailash. There is no effect of cold on them. This thing sat in Siriman's mind. The dream of becoming a mountaineer emerged in his mind. Climbing Mount Kailash became his goal and dream. He passed the matriculation examination at the age of sixteen. Siriman enrolled in an art college. Where he studied about the climber. To become a climber, he would continue to practice the mountain, climbing, landing. After a few years, he completed both his studies and training. Now he was twenty -one years old. He told some of his climber friends- Come on, we went to climb the Mount Kailash. Friends flatly refused. Friends said- till date no mountainous Kailash mountain could climb there. There is always a fear of slipping of snow of that mountain. His friends left from there saying this. But his morale did not diminish. Siriman packed his bag, he went out to climb Mount Kailash alone. He had filled food and drink items and essential items in his bag. A few days later he reached Tibet. He stopped in a rented room in Tibet. It happened in the morning. He went out to climb Mount Kailash after washing his hands and mouth. After some time he reached near Mount Kailash. There was no other person nearby. A sheet of ice was lying everywhere. Siriman saw a white bear. Who was looking at the bag of Siriman with a staring. Siriman fed some food items to that bear. After eating food, the bear left from there. Siriman Mountains started climbing. After some time he reached a high height. Cold winds were blowing. Siriman was going up. Then the ice layer was rubbed at that place. Siriman fell down. Siriman's hands and feet became numb. Siriman was lying there. No person was present around. Then he came there white bear and dragging Siriman. Took a village. The villagers admitted Siriman to a nearby hospital. A few days later his parents came to Tibet to see Siriman. The doctor told Siriman's parents- your son has got paralysis. His entire body is numb. A few years passed. His father died due to some disease. When Siriman heard this, tears flowed in his eyes. Siriman was unable to cremate his father. So his mother cremated him. A few years later, Siriman started to be able to shake his body slowly. The treatment of doctors began to succeed. A few days later he became completely healthy. Siriman took the blessings of his mother and again went out to climb the Kailash mountain. After some time he reached near Mount Kailash. He started climbing the mountain. The shivering cold was spread all around. After some time he climbed the last peak of Mount Kailash. His mind was pleased with happiness. He looked here and there. Neither Shiva appeared there nor anyone else. A thick sheet of snow was seen spreading everywhere. Like the feather, small snow was falling from top. When Siriman looked down from the mountain, he was looking at the white bear from Siriman.

A Spider - A boy named Allen was around eight years old. He belonged to a middle class family. His father was a labourer in a private plant. It was a Sunday. His father was reading the newspaper. His mother was busy cooking. Allen was watching TV. A movie called Spider-Man was being telecast on TV. Allen was watching the movie attentively. As he was watching the movie, wrong information was entering his mind. Allen thought in his mind whether he could also become Spider-Man. The next day his parents had to go out for some important work. That day the boy was alone at home. The thought of becoming Spider-Man was going on in his mind. It was around 9 in the morning. Light winds were blowing in through the window. Allen opened the door and went outside. Sunlight was spread all around. Allen held many types of spiders hanging on the trees in his hand and started moving towards the house. The spiders started biting Allen's hand. Allen started feeling unbearable pain due to the bites of the spiders. Allen's grip started to loosen. The spiders slipped from his hands. He started moaning in pain. After some time he fell unconscious. The sun was very bright. After some time his parents reached there. The parents picked Allen up and took him to the hospital. At that time, desperation and sadness were visible on Allen's parents' faces. Allen was lying on a bed in the hospital. The doctor was treating him. It was evening. The treatment continued for many days. After some days Allen became healthy. Now Allen was free from many kinds of wrong information. Allen developed a kind of fear of spiders in his mind. The parents took Allen in a rented car and started towards their home.

The Bridge - A woman was travelling in a train. She had a precious gold chain around her neck. It was shining in the moonlight. She was very happy. She was going to her home. The woman was standing near the door of the train and watching the scenery outside. Two people saw her gold chain. Greed arose in their mind. Most of the people were asleep at that time. Two people came to the woman and asked for the gold chain from her. The woman flatly refused. Then those two people tried to snatch the chain from the woman. The train was passing through a bridge. In this scuffle, those two people pushed the woman and took the chain from her neck. The woman fell straight into the river. The flow of the river was very fast. The woman was swept away in the strong current of the river screaming and shouting. Both of them were smiling at that woman. After a few days, they were watching TV in their home and were discussing that tonight again a woman should be robbed. It was raining heavily outside. Their house was situated near the river. The house was very old. Perhaps that house was built by their great grandfather. The water level of the river started rising. The water of the river started getting faster. After some time the water of the river took the form of a flood. Their house was destroyed in this terrible flood. Those people and their house got submerged in the fast flow of water.

Drums In The Forest - There was a person named Saru. Saru used to sell coal. His whole family was dependent on him. The money he earned by selling coal was the only source of income for his family. One day Saru went to the mine to get coal. It was summer. The sun was shining brightly. Hot winds were blowing everywhere. He took out coal from the mine, filled it in sacks and started walking towards home. After some time he reached home. It was afternoon. There was a lot of dust stuck to his body. His hands had turned black. He first took a bath and then started eating. After eating, he started taking some rest. It was evening. Saru's cycle was loaded with sacks of coal. He took his cycle and set out to sell coal. The sun had become less bright. He was roaming from village to village. But today his coal was not selling. He became a little sad. He decided to go a little further. There was a village at some distance. To go to that village, one had to cross a small dense forest. Saru was crossing the forest. The chirping of birds was heard. After some time he reached the village. Now the sun had started setting. A voice came from a house. How much is the price of coal? He went to that house. After bargaining, he sold all the coal to that person. It was night. A feeling of happiness appeared on Saru's face. All his coal was sold. He bought a small bottle of liquor from a liquor shop for some money. He had a very old torch. He started going towards home drinking liquor and lighting the torch. The night had become very dark. The moon had come out. Saru looked back and saw torches burning in the village. After some time he got intoxicated. In an intoxicated state, riding a bicycle seemed impossible to him. He started walking towards home with the bicycle. He now reached the forest path. On the way, he saw a person hanging upside down on a tree. Saru started talking to him for some time. But the person hanging upside down was not responding. Saru shone the light of his torch on him. He was stunned. He started trembling with fear. Sweat appeared on his forehead. There was only one head on the tree. Which was hanging upside down on the tree. The torso of that person was lying on the ground below the tree. It seemed that this person had been murdered some time ago. Saru's intoxication had vanished. He started leaving quickly from there in panic on his bicycle. After going some distance, he heard the sound of drums from the right side of the road. Saru's fear went away to some extent. He thought that someone is celebrating in the forest. He kept his bicycle near a tree and started going to the right side of the road. He reached that place. He hid behind a dense tree and started watching everything. Some people were celebrating by dancing around the fire. They had sharp axes, guns and knives in their hands. Some people were playing drums. Seeing all this, Saru became more scared. His forehead started sweating. Seeing them, it seemed that there was a group of bandits celebrating. Seeing all this, Saru's intoxication had gone away. Saru kept walking backwards slowly without making any noise. After going some distance, he ran fast. He soon reached his bicycle. He sat on the bicycle and started going towards home quickly. There was no one on the road. The road was completely deserted. He had now left the jungle path. He reached his village. He felt relieved. He reached near his house. His forehead was covered with sweat. He knocked on the door. His wife opened the door. She was a little nervous. Her husband was completely scared. Saru came inside the house. His wife closed the door. She asked - what happened to you? Saru told everything. The wife thanked God. It was morning. Saru's body was burning with fever. His wife called a nearby doctor. The doctor examined him and prescribed medicines. After a few days, Saru recovered. But whenever Saru remembered that incident, he would shiver. A few weeks later. Saru was sitting on a chair. News was being shown on TV. The news said - A group of bandits living in the forest were killed in a fight.

Gang Of Kidnapers - A city where children were disappearing day by day. Everyone was confused as to how the children were disappearing? One day the intelligence department officials came to know that a gang of kidnappers were taking many children in sacks through the forest. Those officials sent this information to the army soldiers. The army soldiers set out towards the forest to catch the kidnappers. It was afternoon. Hot winds were blowing everywhere. After some time the army soldiers reached there. The soldiers caught all the kidnappers. All the children were taken out of the sacks. All the children had fainted. They were awakened by sprinkling water on them. Those children were handed over to their parents and the kidnappers were handed over to the police. The police started the investigation. The kidnappers told that we kidnap children from different villages and cities. We sell the kidnapped children to the organ dealer at whatever price he asks. After a few days the organ dealer was caught. Police officers started questioning the dealer. The dealer said, "We take out the organs from the bodies of those children and sell them to doctors of big hospitals in India and abroad. We used to take the bodies of the children abroad by ship and bury them in the soil." People working with the organ dealer were also caught. But big people were involved in this case. So, after spending a few days in jail, they were released. Because they had bought the police officers by paying a lot of money. A few weeks passed. The gang of kidnappers again set out to hunt for children. They got down in a pond and started going to the other side. There were electric poles on the banks of that pond and electric wires were hanging on them. The wires were many years old. But high voltage current ran in those wires. They had reached the middle of the pond. The electric wire got loose from the pole and fell into the water. Electricity spread in the water and all the people of that group died in no time. On the other hand, the dealer and the doctor involved in this scandal were afflicted with TB. Due to coughing day and night, their condition started deteriorating day by day. The police officers who had received a huge amount of money as bribe. After a few days, the Income Tax Department officials raided the house of those police officers. After which a huge amount of black money was seized from their house. Those bribe-taking officers were arrested.

The Track - Hundreds of people were travelling in the train. The train was jam packed with passengers. It was morning time. A mild cold breeze was blowing. The train was still quite far from the station. A shepherd was grazing his sheep at some distance from the track. The shepherd's eyes fell on the track which was broken to a large extent. The shepherd was an old man. His hair, beard and moustache had turned white. Without delaying, he ran towards the oncoming train. His breathing was getting fast. His whole body started aching due to fatigue. Now sunlight had started spreading all around. After some time, the shepherd reached quite far. The shepherd saw the oncoming train. The shepherd was wearing a red coloured towel. The shepherd, panting, stood on the track and waved his red towel. The train driver sensed the danger on seeing the red towel and applied emergency brakes. The shepherd moved away from the track. Sparks started coming out due to the dragging of the wheels of the train. After going some distance, the train stopped. Many people got out of the train. After some time, the shepherd reached there. A man got angry and slapped the shepherd. That man had to reach early due to some work. That man thought that this shepherd showed the red towel without any reason. The shepherd got slapped and went away from there without saying anything, taking his sheep. When many people walked some distance, they saw that the track was really broken. That man started regretting his mistake. It was afternoon. After a few days, the government honored the shepherd by giving him an award and that man also apologized to the shepherd.

The Old House - Some children came out of the cinema hall after watching a movie. It was evening. Those children were going towards their home. The sky was cloudy. They were moving forward having fun. Cold winds were blowing. After some time, it started raining. To avoid getting wet, they came near an old house. That house was very old. Some time passed. But the rain was not stopping. Now it was night.
The door of the house was open. They went inside the house. It was very dark inside. There was a sound of the door closing. As if someone

had closed the door. The hearts of the children started beating loudly. It was not possible to see clearly in the dark. The children were locked in the house. Some murderer came running and kept attacking the children with a sharp knife. The screams of the children started echoing. One child ran. He started going upstairs through the stairs. The murderer also started following him. There was a weak glass window in the room upstairs. The child hit the glass window hard. The glass broke and the child fell down with a thud. A police jeep was passing by. Police officers heard the sound. The officers got out of the jeep and ran towards the child. The murderer was staring at the child from the window. The officers looked towards the window. The murderer hid. The officers called an ambulance and sent the child to the hospital. The officers went inside with lights. The floor of the house was red with blood. The dead bodies of the children were lying on the floor. The murderer started running away from there. The police officers fired bullets at him. But he escaped from there. The police officers started searching the entire city. The murderer hid in a very old house deep inside the forest nearby. He remained hidden there for two days. He started celebrating his victory of escaping from the clutches of the officers. He started dancing and jumping loudly on the floor of that old house. Due to which the roof of the house fell on him. He got a deep injury on the head. Blood started flowing. After some time, due to hunger, thirst and excessive bleeding, he stopped breathing. After a few days, his corpse started rotting and a foul smell started spreading. Rats started gnawing the flesh from the body of the corpse.

Motivational Speaker - A boy from a poor family named Tanesh. He was around sixteen years old. Due to poverty, Tanesh had developed the habit of stealing. One day, Tanesh got a chance and entered a man's house. He could not succeed in stealing and was caught. When his father came to know about this, he became very angry. Tanesh's father came there and slapped Tanesh twice. He started crying right there. Tears started falling from his eyes. Everyone went to their respective homes. The next day Tanesh left the house and ran away. This news spread in the entire village. Tanesh was searched for. But he was not found. Tanesh had gone to some faraway district. Tanesh took shelter on a tree and started working at a dhaba. With the money he got from working, he would buy food and eat and save some money. With the saved money, he would buy some books and keep reading. On the other hand, the parents would sit sad at home when they could not find Tanesh. Days went by like this. Five years passed. Tanesh now started working as a motivational speaker on small stages. He earned some money from this. Now he did not go to work at the Dhaba. Slowly he became famous. One day Tanesh's parents had come to the market to buy vegetables. A known person came and said - Your son is acting on stage. Hearing this, a smile came on the faces of the parents. They started moving towards the stage quickly. Thousands of people had gathered around the stage. The father also started watching his son's show. Today the parents were feeling proud seeing their son. After a few hours the show ended. Everyone started going to their respective homes. Tanesh also started moving towards his car. The father did not have the courage to say anything. Both of them started walking towards their home quietly. Tanesh looked towards them. Tanesh recognized his parents. Tanesh came from behind and put his hand on his father's shoulder. The father looked back and saw that it was his son. Who had now become a 22-year-old youth. The son touched his parents' feet and tears of joy appeared in the parents' eyes.

Penance - There was a person named Raghuman. When he was eighteen years old, he left his studies and took blessings from his parents and left for the forest to do penance. He used to do penance by staying in the forest. His parents also did not know which forest their only son had gone to. He used to fill his stomach by eating leaves of trees and plants. He used to quench his thirst by drinking water from lakes and waterfalls. Days passed like this. After a few years, Raghuman's father died. The villagers searched for Raghuman to perform the last rites of his father. But Raghuman was not found. Raghuman's mother performed his last rites. Some days passed. Raghuman was engrossed in his penance. He did not even know that his father had died. His mother mortgaged her house. With the money received from mortgaging, she arranged for a feast. People from the entire village came to the feast. It was evening. Everyone went home after eating. Raghuman's mother was lying on the cot. She was remembering her husband and son. Time passed like this. Now the ration of the house was over. Raghuman's mother started sleeping on an empty stomach. After a few days, Raghuman's mother stopped breathing. The villagers cremated his mother. Forty-two years passed. Even after doing penance for forty-two years, Raghuman could not find God. He was now sixty years old. His hair, beard and moustache had become long and white.

Raghuman had now become old. He came to his village. But people could not recognize him. Raghuman reached his house. The house was locked. Raghuman asked a person - Brother, why is there a lock on this place? And where did the people living here go? The person told him everything. Raghuman came to know that his parents are no longer in this world. He was deeply shocked. Raman sat there and started crying bitterly. Now the house also belonged to the landlord. Raghuman wiped his tears and sat under a banyan tree. He was now regretting. He was thinking to himself. If I wanted, I could have served my parents or lived happily with my parents. But now it was too late. Raghuman no longer had the strength to work. Now he used to sit under the same tree every day. If someone gave him food, he would eat it or if he did not get food, he would remain hungry.

Separation - A movie named Bajrangi Bhaijaan was playing in the cinema hall. Rashm was watching that movie. After the movie was over, he was going home on his motorcycle. It was around 8 o'clock at night. He was passing in front of the railway station. He heard a girl crying. Rashm stopped his motorcycle and went to the station. Rashm saw a 12 year old girl crying calling out for her mother. Rashm asked, "What is your name? Where are you from?" The girl said, "My name is Sharifa. I am from Pakistan. How did that girl get separated from her mother?" She told Rashm all this. Rashm took her to his home. It was morning. Rashm took her to an office where Pakistani visas are made. The Indian official told Rashm, "All the roads leading to Pakistan have been closed for seven days. So you come after seven days." Rashm took Sharifa from there and left. Inspired by the movie Bajrangi Bhaijaan, Rashm started thinking about taking the girl through another route. The next day, Rashm reached the Pakistan border in the west of Rajasthan with the girl. Sand was spread all around. Hot winds were blowing. Rashm started looking for a tunnel here and there. But he could not find the tunnel. Rashm now tried to go to Pakistan by cutting the barbed wires laid on the border. By then Indian soldiers arrived there. Rashm was caught. Rashm was interrogated. Rashm told everything. Rashm's family members reached there after some time. Rashm was released after a few days. The Indian government handed over the little girl to the Pakistan government. The Pakistan government safely delivered the girl to her parents.

A Link - An eighteen year old girl named Sariya who completed her 12th standard a few days ago. Sariya was the only child of her parents. Her parents pampered her a lot. One day Sariya was lying on the bed in her room and was using Facebook. She received a friend request from a boy named Silaun on Facebook. Sariya accepted the friend request. Silaun sent a link to Sariya. Sariya opened her account on a dating app by clicking on the link and installed the app from the play store. They kept talking for a few days. Silaun dated Sariya to have sex. Sariya agreed. It was morning the next day. Sariya got ready and told her mother- Mother I am going for a walk with my friends, I will return in the evening. Saying this Sariya sat in a rented car and reached the address given by Silaun. She went inside the rented room. She saw Silaun was sitting on the bed. Both of them started having sex together. After some time it became evening. Their sex program ended. Both of them went to their respective homes. The next day Sariya woke up. A message came on her mobile. In which it was written- Give me five lakh rupees as soon as possible. Otherwise I will make the sex video viral. You have only two days time. It was Silaun who sent this message. Silaun had taken the video with a hidden camera. Sariya was shocked. She did not understand what to do now? Sariya was from a middle class family. She thought of committing suicide. She hung herself with a noose. She started struggling. Just then her mother came there and held her feet. Because it was Sunday, her father was also at home. Her father came there and brought her down. She was breathing. Sariya was made to sit on the bed. After giving her water, the mother said- Son, why were you doing this? Sariya told everything to her parents. The parents supported Sariya. He filed a report in the police station. Silaun was arrested and put in jail. The police officers beat Silaun badly and took the video from him and deleted it.

The Old Man - Two terrorists were planting bombs on the railway track. At some distance, a shepherd was grazing his sheep. That shepherd was an old man. Whose age was more than sixty years. The terrorists planted a bomb on the track and blew it up. There was a loud sound. The old man said- what happened? People started coming to see this. The terrorists started running from there. Suddenly the weather changed. Dark clouds started gathering. A lightning struck those two terrorists and they fell on the ground. A large part of the track was broken. That old man saw all this. The old man heard the sound of the train from a very far distance. Which was quite far. The old man had a red gamchha around his neck. The old man started running on the railway tracks holding the gamchha. His breathing was getting fast. He got tired and stopped. He started panting. He then ran with all his might. He stopped again and then ran again. While doing this, he came very close to the train. Panting, he waved the red gamchha like a flag. The train driver saw this. The old man stood a little distance away from the track. The train driver applied emergency brakes. The train was about a hundred meters away from the broken track. The wheels of the train were dragging and moving. Sparks started appearing on the tracks due to the friction of the wheels of the train. The train stopped a little distance away from the broken track. Everyone started getting down. The train driver also got down. The train driver saw. The track was badly broken. The train driver muttered to himself and said- if that old man had not been there today, a big accident could have happened. After some time the police came there. Two men were lying there. They were taken to the hospital. The doctors said- both of them have become paralyzed. The search for the old man began. But that old man was not found. Perhaps that old man did not want to take credit for his good deed.

The Crop - A person named Saresh was a farmer. He was married to a girl named Muni.

They had two children. Saresh would wake up every morning, wash his hands and face, eat and then leave to work in the fields. The livelihood of his family depended on farming. Saresh would return home by evening. He belonged to a poor family whose main occupation was farming. He had neither a tractor nor a cow or bull. He only had a wooden plough with which he ploughed the fields. One day Saresh woke up in the morning and went to the field. When he looked in the field, the crop was flourishing. The paddy present in the field had ripened. Looking at the crop present in the field, it seemed that there was a golden colour. The farmer rushed to his home. He told everything to his wife. Saresh and Muni reached the field with harvesting tools. Both of them started harvesting the crop. It was evening. All the crop had been harvested. Both of them filled the crop in sacks and took it home. The next day they started threshing the crop. After a few hours, the paddy was separated from the crop. He took a machine on rent. He took out rice from the paddy with the machine and returned the machine. He filled the rice in sacks. Next day, the farmer went to sell the sacks of rice to a government official. The government official told the farmer that I can give you only fifty rupees. Saresh knew that he was trying to cheat me. The value of so much rice was much more than fifty rupees. When Saresh protested, the official slapped him twice. Saresh stood there sadly. He started shedding tears. A person made a video of this scene and uploaded it on social media. Slowly, this scene spread all over the country. Slowly, all the farmers started protesting. All the farmers of the country started supporting Saresh. All the farmers of the country stopped farming and participated in the movement. Some days passed. The government ration stock started getting exhausted slowly. The economic activity of the country started deteriorating. The price of food items of the country kept increasing day by day. People were unable to buy it. The Prime Minister of the country decided to meet Saresh. The Prime Minister came to Saresh. Saresh told the entire matter to the Prime Minister. The Prime Minister called that officer here and asked him to apologize. The officer apologized to Ramesh with folded hands. The Prime Minister told his officers- this misbehaving officer should be removed from his post. After that there was an echo of applause there. The Prime Minister sat in his car and left from there. The movement ended. Saresh sold his rice to the government at a reasonable price. Time passed. Slowly the government ration stores started filling up. Economic activities started becoming normal and the prices of food items started becoming normal.

Electric Reet - When a transgender girl was born, her parents named her Reet. Then all the people in the neighborhood tried to convince Reet's parents to hand over the child to the transgenders. But they ignored their words and decided to raise the child. Slowly Reet started growing up. She was admitted to a school. She was now six years old. The teachers in the class would make Reet sit on the last bench, away from everyone. The children would make fun of her. Sometimes she would cry and tears would come out of her eyes. No student would talk to her, play with her or stay with her. Every other day, sometimes the people in the neighborhood would scold Reet's parents. Due to which they would become sad. Reet would come home crying and hug her parents. Then her parents would encourage Reet. Days went by like this. Reet was now twelve years old. Reet now spent most of her time reading books. She had a special interest in mathematics and physics. Now books had become Reet's friends. Some years passed. She completed her tenth, eleventh and twelfth grades. She now started studying engineering. After some years she completed her graduation, post graduation and PhD. She had now received her doctorate. She had now become Dr. Reet. She was now twenty-six years old. She now spent most of her time in making something new. Some days passed. Reet thought of making an electric rocket. So that the rocket does not spread pollution and the environment remains pollution free. Reet prepared the method and model of the rocket design. She went to the country's space authorities. She told everything about it. The officials agreed. After five years the electric rocket was ready. On the day of the rocket test, many countrymen came to see the test. The rocket was launched. After flying some distance, the rocket fell down and blasted. The test failed. Reet felt a kind of shock. The officers scolded Reet and sent her away. Reet's father was shocked by his daughter's failure. He had a heart attack and could not survive. When Reet came home, she saw that her father was lying on the bier and her mother was crying bitterly. Tears started flowing from Reet's eyes. One was the sorrow of failure and the other was the sorrow of her father's death. Reet felt both the sorrows together. Her father's body was cremated. Reet was now sad and worried. A few months passed. Now her mother controlled herself and encouraged Reet. Days passed like this. One day the officers were checking the CCTV camera. Then they saw an engineer named Lalima removing many machines from the electrical rocket. The officers came to know why the rocket test was not successful. The officers regretted their mistake and went to Reet. They apologized to Reet and told her everything. The authorities said to Reet- please make an electric rocket again. Reet agreed. After a few years Reet made an electric rocket again. This time too people came to see the test. The rocket was launched. The rocket flew successfully. The test was successful. Reet's name started getting heard everywhere. All the countrymen were now calling Reet as Electric Reet. Those who used to scold her mother. Today they were respecting her. Reet's father was not with her in this moment of success. Reet looked towards the sky and said to herself- missing you dad.

Repentance - A boy named Lalam. He was from a poor family. His father used to sell coal. His mother used to tell Lalam daily that son, study, go to school. But Lalam did not listen to her. He used to go to school only sometimes and did not study at home. He used to be busy playing and roaming around with his friends. Lalam's friends were from middle class families. Their fathers were employed in government offices. Lalam's father used to go to bring and sell coal only sometimes and the rest of the days he used to remain drunk. The time for examination came. Lalam gave the examination. But due to not studying, he failed in the examination. Days and years passed like this. Lalam was now eighteen years old. Lalam's father did not go to bring and sell coal anymore. His father was now always drunk. Lalam's friends had now become businessmen. Because his friends had enough money. Lalam now used to go to bring and sell coal daily. One day Lalam tied five sacks on his bicycle and set out towards the mine to bring coal. It was summer season. After some time he reached the mine. The mine was quite old. He parked his cycle and started filling coal in sacks. There was scorching sunshine all around. Sweat was dripping from Lalam's forehead. Hot winds were blowing. Some motorcycles were seen coming on the road. The boys riding the motorcycles asked Lalam- How are you Lalam? Lalam said- I am fine. Those motorcycles went on their way. Lalam's friends were riding those motorcycles. Lalam kept staring at the motorcycles as they went. It was afternoon. Lalam filled the coal in sacks and after loading the sacks on the bicycle, he started thinking to himself. If only I had listened to my mother, then today I would not be digging coal. Today he was regretting it. He kept moving towards his home with his bicycle, cursing his life.

Government Hostel - Many children had come to a government hostel after passing the Navodaya examination conducted in government schools. Once while playing in the ground, two boys named Sanan and Gaman got into a fight over something. Gaman was a little stronger. So Sanan knocked Gaman down in the fight. After this scuffle, Sanan felt like taking revenge from Gaman. Both of them were around fifteen years old. Some days passed. It was Sunday. Every Sunday, the hostel allowed children to watch TV for entertainment. There were many big rooms in the same hostel. There were many beds in those rooms. One of those rooms was considered haunted by people. A child had died in that room for some reason. That room was located on the second floor and it was closed for many years. But today someone had opened that room. It was night time. The children in the hostel were watching TV. The clock was around ten o'clock. Sanan had gone to the market in the morning and brought a claw. Its claw was pointed and sharp. A senior child watching TV said to Gaman- You go and call Sanan. He will also watch TV for some time. When Sanan came to know that Gaman was coming to call me, he went to the room on the second floor and sat down covering himself with a blanket. He went to Sanan's room, but he did not find Sanan. He thought that maybe he had gone to the room upstairs. Gaman reached the room on the second floor via the stairs. He crossed three beds and went a little ahead. He saw someone covered with a blanket. He said- Come on, let's go watch TV. Even after calling several times, there was no response. Then Gaman turned and started to go out of the room, when Sanan covered with a blanket ran and caught Gaman from behind and dug his claws on his hand. Gaman thought that he was a ghost and pushed him hard and ran away from there. There were claw marks on his hands. They looked like nail marks. Sanan thought. Now the children and teachers can come here to investigate. So Sanan also ran away from there. Gaman's hand had become completely red and blood had started coming out of his hand. When the children and teachers saw this, they all got scared. Gaman was not able to utter a word due to fear. Everyone went to that room. But there was no one there. Gaman and everyone thought that this is the work of some ghost. In the morning, the parents came and took Gaman home. Sanan was saved by the ghost. Sanan was standing on the roof and was smiling to himself seeing Gaman going.

Salo - Something Different - In Salo or The 120 Days of Sodom, you saw four rich men

imprisoning several boys and girls in a mansion and torturing them and finally killing them all mercilessly. After killing them, the guards started dancing. There was a lot of blood splattered on the veranda and the corpses of the boys and girls were lying there. There was not a single piece of clothing on the corpses. Many body parts of those corpses were cut and scattered on the ground. After some time, on the orders of the rich men, that mansion was blown up with dynamite. They kept the remaining dynamite in their jeep. They all sat in their cars and started going towards the city. The guards were trying to burn the dynamite kept in the jeep and throw it away. Just then there was a huge explosion and the guards were blown to pieces. The cars stopped. After mourning for some time, those rich men, their wives and Stuarts started moving forward. There were many petrol tanks on the truck and Stuarts were riding on it. One Stuart lit his cigarette and started smoking it. At the same time, the truck passed over a speed breaker. Due to which the burning cigarette fell on the petrol tank. The tank on which the burning cigarette fell was open. Due to which the fierce fire engulfed those four Stuarts in no time. The truck stopped. They started burning in the blazing fire, started writhing in pain, started screaming and shouting. Those rich men and their wives started watching this scene. After some time they calmed down. The truck also burnt completely. They sat in their car and started going towards the city. After seeing these scenes, they started sweating due to the fear of death. Leaving their wives there, they sat in their car and started moving towards the city at a fast speed. At some distance from the road, the road was being leveled by a road roller. That car became uncontrollable due to high speed and collided with the road roller. Due to this collision, the driver of the road roller fell into the grass. Slowly the car started getting crushed by the road roller. Along with that, those rich men also started getting crushed in pain. After some time, those four rich men died a painful death. Blood was splattered on the road and their crushed bodies were lying there. Flies were buzzing on them. On the other hand, their wives steal another truck and start driving it. But due to not being able to drive the truck, it falls down from the bridge and overturns. Due to this accident, they get seriously injured, but their lives are saved.

Dying To Live - Motilal ji. He had three daughters. Sumu, Asha and Beli. All three daughters were married. Even after many years, Asha ji did not have any children. Asha ji treated her elder sister's sons and daughters like her own children and loved them. Asha ji's husband had a serious illness. Due to which he could not survive for many years. Now she was alone. But she did not give up the desire to live and decided to live life well. She started living with her elder sister. They already had a cow. She bought a couple of goats. After a few days, she started making and selling muri (puffed rice) from rice. She started collecting the money received from selling muri. After many years, when enough money was collected, she would go with other women to visit and worship in temples located in far off places. The first journey she made was from Jharkhand to Tamil Nadu. Where many grand temples were located. The second journey she made was from Jharkhand to Uttar Pradesh. Where a temple named Kashi was situated. The third journey she took with her younger sister and her children was from Delhi to Jammu and Kashmir. Where the Vaishno Devi temple was situated. The fourth journey she took was from Jharkhand to Nepal. Even today she goes to fairs in the scorching sun and sells food items. She collects money and dreams of visiting new temples and new places.

The Rat Island - The people of the country were troubled by the damage caused by rats. The government of that country found a solution to get rid of the rats. As a solution, the government said that the rats present in the country will be released on an island. Foreigners can also release rats in large numbers on this island. They just have to pay a small amount. Slowly, rats started being released on that island. Everything was fine for a few months. But with the passage of time, the number of rats on that island increased to more than a lakh and their number kept increasing.

That island was spread over just a few kilometers. It was as if the government had left them to die. There was neither rice nor wheat on that island. There were some coconut trees there and sand spread far and wide. Due to lack of food and a very large number, the rats went mad with hunger. The rats present in lakhs nibbled at other creatures living on that island and some rats were even nibbling at some parts of their own bodies. A team to release the rats reached there. They got very scared seeing the scene there. Lakhs of rats were looking angrily at the team. Lakhs of rats came forward to attack them. They tried to run away. But by then lakhs of rats attacked them and started gnawing. They started shouting loudly. After some time the shouting stopped. The government banned releasing rats on the island and the government was forced to completely ban going to that island. That island became famous as Rat Island. But a few days after this incident, a terrible storm came on that island and a large number of rats were killed. But some rats who had not gone mad and were good. Who somehow filled their stomachs by eating coconut leaves. They somehow reached the shore by floating. Due to rising water level, that island got submerged in the sea.

Perin - A girl named Perin came home a few years ago after completing her college studies. Her father worked abroad. Therefore, he rarely came home. Her mother had died. Perin had no siblings. Therefore, she lived alone in her big house. She did not lack anything. Her father used to transfer money to her account every month. She felt lonely in her house. After completing her college studies, she started spending most of her time watching porn videos. Slowly, time passed. Now, after eating, she would only watch porn videos and masturbate. She became mentally ill after watching porn videos for many hours every day. She went out of the house and went to a public place and started taking off her clothes. People were watching this scene and making videos. Perin took off all her clothes and started masturbating in front of people. All the people were laughing loudly after seeing Perin. Police officers came there and took Perin with them.

After reaching the police station, instead of dressing her, the officers made her take a Viagra pill and started having sex with her. This went on for several hours. One by one, everyone satisfied their lust. Perin was still naked. The staff working in the mental asylum was called. Perin was sent with them. The staff lost their temper on seeing Perin and started having sex with her one by one. After some time, they reached the mental asylum. Perin was still not dressed. The staff caught hold of her and started moving towards the electric room. Perin started feeling a lot of pain in her vagina. She had now regained consciousness to a great extent. She was screaming. Leave me. But due to Perin's behavior a few hours before, the staff considered her to be insane. On the other hand, her video was going viral. Perin was made to sit in the electric chair and was tied tightly. As soon as the staff pressed the button to give electric shock, Perin screamed loudly and woke up from her sleep. Her forehead was covered with sweat. She started looking around. She was in her room and the clock was almost three in the night. She drank the water kept nearby. She realized that it was just a nightmare. She fell asleep mumbling in her mind, "Dark Sex".

The Prank - A YouTuber named Janav used to upload prank videos on his YouTube channel.

Due to which people faced a lot of problems. Due to his pranks, many people did not even help the needy people thinking it to be a prank. He was also abused by people many times. But he did not improve. But Janav used to donate fifty percent of the money earned through his channel to the children of the orphanage. Due to which the children of the orphanage used to bow down to him and give him blessings. Once Janav was planning to make a prank video at night. That night a small bulb was burning there. Two men were coming on a bike. There were speed breakers at that place on the road. The man sitting behind had a pistol for safety. They were coming slowly. Then Janav appeared in front of them wearing a scary costume in the darkness of the night and started moving towards them. Both the men got very scared. Only the bike's light and a small bulb were burning there. The man sitting behind the bike was so scared that he fired three bullets at him from his pistol. Seeing all this, the cameraman ran away from there. Janav fell down. Those men rode the bike and fled from there at a fast speed. At the last moment, Janav started remembering his parents. While remembering, tears suddenly appeared in his eyes. He was lying there and counting his few breaths. Just then a jeep of police officers was passing by. The police officers saw him. Without any delay, the officers admitted Janav to the hospital. After some time, his parents reached the hospital. The mother was crying continuously for her son. It was morning. The doctor said- He is fine now. You bring these medicines. Janav's father went to get the medicines. Janav's mother thought. I will bring some food items. Thinking this, the mother went to the market to get food items. The sun was shining everywhere. The mother was bringing food. Then due to extreme sadness, anxiety, fatigue and insomnia, she had a heart attack. She fell down holding her chest with her hand. There was so much mischief in the city that everyone thought that she was also doing mischief like her son and no one helped her. After half an hour, the father reached there searching for his wife. The father picked her up and took her to the hospital with the help of a car. After examining her for some time, the doctor said - See ease no more. The doctor said sorry - If you had brought her a little earlier, she could have been saved. On receiving the news of his mother's death, tears started flowing from Janav's eyes while lying on the bed. After a few months, Janav became completely healthy. After a few days, when Janav came to know that his mother had died because of his bad mischief, he started crying bitterly holding his head. After that, Janav stopped making mischief videos and started making comedy videos. After a few years, he got a lot of fame due to comedy. Sometimes Janav would get sad remembering his mother. But today he was making millions of people laugh by drowning himself in sadness.

Madness - Segwi and Remak were childhood friends and neighbours. Segwi did not study well and Remak was very sharp in studies. Due to which he was the most promising and studious boy in his school. When Segwi failed in the board exams many times. After which she started getting very annoyed with Remak. Even after a few years, Segwi remained in the eighth class and Remak completed her studies till 12th. After a few days, Segwi got fed up with studies and started thinking something. After thinking a lot, a mischievous plan was born in Segwi's mind. Which was going to prove to be a big madness. The next day, Segwi wore black clothes, covered her face with a black cloth and took out a real pistol from the cupboard and set out to complete her plan. That pistol belonged to her father who was a police officer. It was evening time, Remak was returning home on his bicycle, then Segwi stopped Remak and pointed the pistol at him. Seeing the pistol, Remak's heart was beating loudly. Segwi said - Will you have sex with me? Otherwise I will shoot you. Segwi had sex with her at the gunpoint and after some time she left from there as if nothing had happened. Remak returned home but he did not tell anything to his family members due to shame. After a few months, Segwi again gave the exam without studying but this time also she failed. Segwi thought that if I have sex with a very intelligent and successful person, then I will also become a intelligent and successful girl. Segwi now understood that one cannot become knowledgeable without acquiring knowledge. Her mind did not become intelligent but she definitely got pregnant due to having sex without using a condom. When her family members came to know, Segwi was scolded a lot but Segwi did not tell anyone about the naughty act done by her. After nine months, Segwi gave birth to a child. A few weeks after the birth, her family members handed over the child to the parents. Who had no children. A few days after that, Segavi got married in a hurry. Segavi regretted her mistake. She kept worrying about her child and many times her eyes became moist while thinking. On the other hand, Remak also married a studious girl. Even today, while sleeping at night, Remak keeps thinking who that girl was and why did she do that?

Bhelora - In ancient times, there used to be a palace at a place called Bhelora. Which was surrounded by mountains and forests. The princess of the palace was very beautiful. Many servants worked in the palace. One servant whose name was Gairol. He often used to stare at the princess while she was coming and going. The princess also used to see Gairol often. Both of them were more than eighteen years old. Slowly, time passed and their affection grew. It was night time. The princess was sitting outside the palace, waiting for Gairol. Just then her uncle came and forcibly tried to molest the princess. After some time Gairol reached there. Seeing this scene, Gairol became furious. There was a lot of scuffle between Kaka Sa and Gairol. Due to which Deen got injured. The police reached there. The police caught Gairol and took him away from there and the princess did not say anything. On the insistence of the family, the princess gave false testimony in the court. Due to which Gairol was sentenced to ten years. After a few days, the princess went to meet Gairol. Gairol said- Why did you do this? The princess said- For the pride and honor of my family. Please forgive me. After that the princess left from there. After hearing this, sparks of anger started burning in Gairol's eyes. On the other hand, the princess got a kind of complicated disease. Due to which she suffered from that disease for ten years. After completing ten years, Gairol was released from jail. After so many years, the princess also became healthy after getting treatment from many doctors. After a few days, the princess's wedding took place. Bhelora was shining with lights everywhere. There was happiness everywhere. Then a news comes that someone has tied a rope to the feet of the groom who was to marry the princess and hung him from a tree and cut off his genitals. Blood was dripping from the cut genitals. That groom was admitted to the hospital. After which his life was saved. But the atmosphere of the wedding now turned into an atmosphere of mourning. Slowly time passed. Similarly, many grooms who were to marry the princess had the same fate. Now no one wanted to marry the princess. One day, the princess received a letter. It was written in the letter - Your marriage will remain incomplete, your Gairol. The princess got a shock after reading this. A report was filed in the police station. The search for Gairol began. Now the princess would sit sad and silent. One day, fed up with all this, the princess decided to take a wrong step. She reached a deserted bridge. Dressed up like a bride. She kept looking at the water of the river flowing under the bridge for some time and then jumped into the river. When Gairol came to know about this, he was drowned in deep remorse. After some time, he also reached near that bridge. Tears were flowing from his eyes. Light cold winds were blowing. After a few minutes, Gairol also jumped into that river. After shouting for some time, everything became quiet. Now it was evening and both of them were floating in the strong current of the river.

Hope To Reach Home - A driver, a 12 or 13 year old boy, the boy's elder brother and a friend of the elder brother, were travelling in a vehicle. They were going to a wedding for a feast. It was night time. After a few hours they reached the wedding. After eating the feast, they all strolled around for a while in the wedding. After that they got on the vehicle and started going towards home. After travelling some distance, the vehicle stopped. Perhaps there was some problem with the vehicle. It was going to be morning after some time. It was 4:30 in the night. Everyone got down from the vehicle. The driver looked at the vehicle for some time and tried to fix it. But he could not fix the vehicle and started looking for a mechanic. After some time, it was morning. The driver came near the vehicle and said - I could not find a mechanic. They all started looking here and there. They were in a village where there was silence. There were many huts in the village. But apart from them, there was no other person in that village. There was a cot lying near a hut. They lifted the cot and the boy and his brother's friend sat on it. There was liquor and petrol in a big can in the vehicle. The boy's elder brother secretly started drinking liquor in bottles one after the other. When the driver saw this, he also drank some liquor. The boy's elder brother got drunk and started taking off his clothes and went and lay down in front of the wall of the hut wearing only his underwear. The driver also went and slept there. It was as if he was not worried about going home. Due to the summer season, the sun was very strong. Sunlight was spread all around and hot winds were blowing. The owner of the vehicle, that is, the boy's elder brother's friend was very angry. He could not control his anger and in anger, he took out the petrol present in the vehicle and set them on fire. The boy got scared seeing this and ran away from there. He kept running until he was far away from there. On the other hand, due to the fire, both of them died in agony. As soon as the owner of the vehicle sat on the cot, a poisonous snake bit him. The owner of the vehicle tried to run away from here. But his foot hit a stone. While trying to control himself, he caught hold of a hanging wire. After which, due to high voltage current, he died in a short time. That boy would stop and then run, then stop and then run. While doing this, he reached a city. His breathing was fast. He was tired and had also forgotten the way home. He sat under a tree and started looking around in fear. A lot of time passed. That boy spent the night climbing a tree. It was morning. The sounds of birds and vehicles started coming. He woke up from sleep. He was very hungry. But he had neither food nor money. He plucked leaves from the tree and ate as much as he could. When he remembered his home, tears suddenly appeared in his eyes. He came down from the tree and started running. He did not know where he was going. He was just hoping that he would reach home someday.

Siya Alive - You saw in the movie Siya that on the pretext of giving a job to a village girl named Siya, an MLA makes love to her. After a few days, the MLA's son and some of his friends kidnap Siya from the road and rape her for several days in a deserted house. The police arrest those boys with evidence. The MLA's son and his friends are left on bail and Siya takes help from one of her friends, who was a lawyer, to get justice. When the MLA comes to know about this, the MLA's men take Siya's father out and beat him up so much that he leaves him half dead. After a few days, Siya's uncle is also taken away by the police officers. A few days ago, this case was handed over to the CBI. That's why the MLA was scared. After suffering so much, Siya's father could not survive. Fearing the possibility of getting punished for murder, Siya's father is burnt alive at night on the orders of the MLA. After that, Siya, her mother, her aunt and lawyer were going to the court in a taxi. Then a truck hits them. After which Siya gets injured and everyone else is killed. On the other hand, Siya is lying on the hospital bed. After a few days, Siya regains consciousness. Outside the room, her younger brother and CBI officers were waiting for her. After questioning by those officers, Siya starts resting. After a few hours, it becomes night. Siya peeks outside the room and sees that all the CBI officers have left from there. Siya leaves from there with her younger brother. After walking for several hours, they had come quite far from there. They saw an orphanage. They sat under a tree near that orphanage. In the morning, when the orphanage opened, Siya left her younger brother in the orphanage and went from there. After walking for several hours, she went several kilometers away from that village. The case was closed as Siya ran away. Siya went to a small forest. She started living on top of a tree. Day by day Siya's anger was increasing. When she felt hungry, she would chew the leaves of the tree. She had heard about dynamite from somewhere. A dangerous plan was born in her mind. She would sleep during the day and at night she would go from village to village and steal dynamite from the fishermen. Sometimes she would steal dynamite from factories as well. When more than ten kilos of dynamite would accumulate, Siya would take those dynamite and fit it under the walls of the MLA's house and cover it with soil. While doing this, her body would start aching due to fatigue. While doing this, about six months passed and the day came when more than a hundred kilos of dynamite were fitted. Siya connected the dynamite to the control box. She tried to activate it. All the dynamite was connected by an electric wire. It was a dark night. The MLA, his men, his son, his son's friends, the women of the house and small children were also present in that house. Siya kept trying the whole night. But the dynamite did not activate. It was morning. Some police officers were passing by and they saw Siya. The officer started taking Siya away from there and said in a loud voice - you all will not touch anything here. But that day everyone was in deep sleep. So no one heard properly. The officer left from there with Siya and the search team was called. After some time the women and children got ready and went to worship in the temple. A man of the house started going towards the back of the house to urinate. He was still half asleep. The rest of the members of the house were still in deep sleep. There were dark clouds in the sky and there was also a mild thunder. While walking towards the back of the house, his foot hit the control box and the button to activate the dynamite got pressed. Due to which the dynamite got activated and an explosion occurred. Due to which the house collapsed in a short time. The person whose foot hit the box also died by getting buried under the debris of the house. All the people present in the house died due to the explosion and the debris of the destroyed house. Some time ago, Siya was cursing God in her mind. But when she got the news of the house getting destroyed and the death of the criminals, she became happy. On the other hand, the MLA's wife was feeling very remorseful because she remained silent even after knowing the evil deeds of her son and husband. Siya was presented in the court. The MLA's wife came to the court and told the whole truth. After which the MLA, his men, his son and his friends were declared criminals. The court sentenced Siya to a few years of imprisonment for stealing dynamite, trying to destroy the house with dynamite, and not killing anyone. Siya was released after completing the sentence. Siya reached the ashram after walking for several hours. The younger brother, on seeing his elder sister, hugged her and started crying loudly. It was evening. The sun was about to set after some time. Siya started walking towards her village holding her younger brother's hand.

The Unknown Village - Sunida, who became a new teacher a few days ago, was extremely happy. She was extremely happy. But the school where she was appointed was quite far from the city. The next day, she was leaving after taking her father's blessings when her father said - Daughter, take some change with you. It will be useful for you. Sunida said - Father, I will take change from someone outside. After that she left the house. She started walking towards the bus stop. After some time she reached near the bus stop. She caught the bus and started walking towards the school. There is an unknown village before that school. When Sunida searched the name of the school on the map of the smartphone, it came up. But there was no information available on the map about that unknown village located a little distance from the school or maybe no one had left any information. She was a little surprised to see this. After a few hours, the bus started passing through that village. When Sunida looked out of the window, she felt a little nervous. There was no shop in that village. People sitting outside were just looking at Sunida. It was as if their eyes were fixed on Sunida only. Sunida closed the window of the bus and started listening to some songs on her smartphone. After some time the bus reached near the school. Sunida got down from the bus and started going towards the school. A child from the school started running with Sunida's smartphone. Sunida also started running after him. In this running around her smartphone got broken. Other teachers also went there. Sunida felt bad. But still she forgave that child. Sunida shows them her appointment letter and introduces herself. After that she goes to the class and starts teaching. During the lunch break when Sunida was having food. That boy sitting on the bench next to Sunida said - Maam I am sorry. After that that boy said - Maam you should leave from here before night and if you ever have to stay here at night then under no circumstances do not open your door at night. Sunida said - Why. The boy was about to speak now when the bell rang. That boy went to his class. Sunida thought. He must be joking. They did not pay much attention to what that boy said. School closed in the afternoon. Sunida started waiting for the bus. A teacher asked Sunida - Can I drop you somewhere? Sunida said - The bus is about to come, I will go by bus.

The rest of the teachers started towards their homes in their vehicles. But Sunida did not know that the bus had already left today. The bus used to return in the evening. But due to some work, the bus had already left today. There was no house near the school. It was evening. But not the bus. After seeing those people, Sunida did not have the courage to go to that unknown village. Slowly the evening started setting. Sunida decided to stay in the school today. She gathered courage and broke the lock of the class with a stone and went inside. She closed the doors and windows properly from inside. It was night. The sounds of insects and jackals were coming. Sunida lay down on a bench. After some time there was a knock on the door. Hearing the knocking sound Sunida got up and sat on the bench. The first time she did not open the door, the second time also she did not open the door. But the third time she heard someone knocking she thought. Maybe someone is in some trouble. Thinking this she opened the door. She was shocked to see outside. Around fifty people were standing outside and they were just looking at Sunida. Sunida tried to close the door but by then one man caught her. The other man tied her mouth tightly with a cloth. Those people took off Sunida's clothes one by one. Those people picked up Sunida and took her to a deserted place. Those people started raping Sunida one by one. After some time Sunida died. Blood started dripping from her vagina. They did not even leave Sunida's dead body. The remaining people started having sex with the dead body. After a few hours, when their lust was satiated, they threw Sunida's body in a deep pit. When the police inquired, neither any villager nor any school employee told anything. Due to fear, they were making up false stories and telling them to the police officer. When the police could not find anything after the inquiry, they closed the case and wrote 'missing' on Sunida's posters and pasted them on the walls. After a few years, a virus spread in that village. All the hundreds of people in that village, except for fifty people, became fine. But the surprising thing was that those fifty villagers were taking the doctor's medicines, but instead of reducing, the disease was increasing. The doctors were also surprised by this. Those fifty villagers started vomiting blood and the skin of their bodies started to peel off slowly. They were having unbearable pain. They were telling the doctor - kill us. But the doctor could not do that. He died after suffering for a few days.

First Attempt - Nasaki, a 23-year-old farmer's son. When he was young, an IAS officer had come to his village. Everyone was respecting that officer. Since then, Nasaki had a desire to become an IAS officer. Nasaki's mother had died in his childhood. After completing graduation, Nasaki started preparing for UPSC. He did not have enough money to go to the city and study. So he thought of studying from home. He used to study for two and a half hours in the morning and two and a half hours in the evening. His friends would tell him, "Hey friend, at least give the exam." But he would say - I will give the exam only after preparing well. After a few days. When Nasaki went out, many people would say about him - Boys who go out and take tuitions are not able to pass the UPSC exam and this farmer's son will pass the exam by studying from home. These things used to hurt Nasaki. But still he would calmly walk away from there. After about 7 years. Nasaki had read more than 25 books related to the exam. He was now 30 years old. The day Nasaki was going to give the exam, bank and police officials came and took his father away. Because his father had taken a loan of 25 thousand rupees from the bank for his son's education. But in this inflation, he was not able to repay the loan on time. Already the house and farm land were mortgaged to someone else. Nasaki's eyes became moist. He became sad. But still he went to the city and gave the UPSC exam. After a few months. Nasaki had passed both the exams in the first attempt itself. There was no limit to his happiness. But still one thing was left. That was the interview. When Nasaki went to the police station and told this news to his father, tears of joy appeared in his father's eyes. Nasaki used to go to meet his father sometimes. After a few weeks, he had to go for an interview. He kept trying by watching several interview videos on YouTube platform on his smartphone. The day of the interview came. Nasaki got ready and went for the interview. The interview went well. The officers taking the interview said - You have cleared the interview. But there are less seats and more students. Therefore, you will have to give us at least five lakh rupees. Only then can you become an IAS officer. Nasaki spontaneously said - bribe. The officers said - yes brother, whatever you call it. If you are able to arrange five lakhs after a few days, then your seat is confirmed, otherwise leave from here right now. Nasaki started leaving from there with a sad face. The officers were saying - there is no money in the pocket and you are going to become an IAS. Nasaki was sitting under the street light at night and looking at the trees and plants. Tears were coming out of his eyes and were dripping down. In the morning. He caught a bus to his village and went to his home. He did not tell his father about these things because he did not want to make his father sad. He started earning his livelihood by working as a labourer for several months. After one year, when Nasaki was drinking tea, he saw a newspaper hanging on the shop. He started reading that newspaper. It was written in it that CBI raided the house of the officers who took the interview. Crores of rupees of black money was seized from their house and they have been suspended from their posts. They have also been arrested. After knowing this, Nasaki started laughing loudly and started running towards his house. He started studying again and gave the exam again this time. Nasaki passed the exam in the second attempt as well. He also passed the interview. After a few years of training, he returned to his village as an IAS officer. The villagers were honoring him and garlanding him with flowers. A month later, after repaying the bank loan, he releases his father and starts taking him to his new home.

Motherhood - Lalita Devi was born in a small village. She had two sisters and six brothers. During her childhood, Lalita was going to school. Her eyes fell on a girl named Khoma. Khoma's father was employed in B.C.C.L. He had a good salary. Khoma used to go to school every day wearing different clothes and slippers. Lalita was surprised to see her pomp and show. Lalita used to play games with her brothers and sisters, celebrate festivals. After studying for a few years, Lalita left her studies. She had studied till sixth or seventh standard. She now used to do household work. After a few years, when she became eligible for marriage, her parents got her married to a man named Shankar. The income of the house was not good. Shankar ji's father used to go to work for some days and the rest of the days he used to remain drunk. Shankar ji used to sell coal. After about a year, they had a son. But after a few years, the child could not survive because he suffered from jaundice. This made Lalita ji sad. The second time her child was born, he was in a critical condition. The doctors tried to save him but he could not be saved. Lalita ji was again sad. Tears rolled down the eyes of the parents. Other family members suggested that the dead child be buried a little distance from the river under the bridge. The dead child was buried. After that, a third child was born. This time a girl was born. There was a wave of happiness in the house. At that time Lalita ji had five sisters-in-law. Some of them were married. But those who were married, used to stay less at their husband's house and used to stay at their parents' house for many months and years. Because here they did not have to work much. Also, their children also lived with them. Lalita ji had to work more. The sisters-in-law used to work less and rest more. One day her daughter went to the ration shop to buy biscuits. She did not have money. So she asked the ration shop owner for a biscuit worth fifty paise on credit. But the ration shop owner refused and drove her away. She went to her mother crying. Then her mother bought her biscuits. About one or two years later, the fourth child was born. But the condition of that child was also serious. After treatment by doctors, the condition of that child improved a bit. After a few weeks, the doctors prescribed medicines and advised to keep this child in front of the light of a bulb. At that time there was no electricity in village. So they decided to take that child to the house of the eldest sister-in-law. The elder sister-in-law lived in her in-laws' house, which was located in Dhanbad district. Her husband worked in BCCL and there was electricity in their house. The child was kept at the elder sister-in-law's house for about one and a half months. The father used to come to meet him occasionally. Many times Lalita ji went with her husband to show the child to the doctor. When the child became healthy, he was brought home. A few months passed. Lalita ji's husband left the job of selling coal and fish and started a hardware shop with the money he had saved. After about five years,

Lalita ji had a fifth child. That child did not have any serious disease. But in childhood, he used to have pain in his ears many times. Due to which he would start crying loudly. Shankar ji would try to pacify him by picking up the child in his lap. Hearing the child's crying voice, the mother also felt like crying. After getting treatment from the doctor, his ear pain got cured in a few months. After about two years, the sixth child was born. He also did not have any serious disease. But a disease called Pachis troubled him a bit. Which got cured later. That sixth child was seven or eight years old. At that time, when his mother would bring food to him, many times he would lie and get his mother scolded by his father. Even then the mother would forgive that child. When their daughter became eligible for marriage, she was married with great pomp and show. After a few years, the sixth boy became mentally ill. He was taken to many tantriks and doctors. But he did not get cured. This increased the worry of the parents. But after a few years, he came out of the mental illness. About seven years after the daughter's marriage, her husband committed suicide due to fear of corona disease. That daughter had now become a widow. Lalita ji and her family members started crying. On the other hand, the daughter who was in her in-laws' house got a shock. She had two children.

She was worried from inside about how she would raise her small children. After this incident, many times tears would appear in the eyes of the parents thinking about their daughter and her children. The mind would become sad. But the parents supported their daughter wholeheartedly. Their daughter stayed in her maternal home for many months. After that she went to her in-laws' house. Lalita ji used to worry about her daughter and her children. When her grandchildren came to her house. She would pamper them. She would fulfill their small desires. She would send food to them.

College Delinquent - Teachers' Day was being celebrated in the college. Many students decided to spend the night in the college. In the morning, when the teachers and students reached the college courtyard, they were terrified to see the scene there. There was a dead body lying in the courtyard and it was of a student studying in the college who was celebrating Teachers' Day party last night. It looked like he had been stabbed several times in the stomach. A lot of blood was scattered on the ground. After some time, the police officers were informed and they took the body with them. People present in the college were also questioned. The next day, three brothers came to the city with their father. The college was in the city itself. The student whose dead body was found in the college was a friend of his elder brother. The younger brother loved to watch detective movies. He was around 18 years old. Being a friend of the elder brother, the younger brother reached the college and started investigating. Somehow he got a clue about the culprit. It was afternoon. The ground was also getting hot due to the scorching sun. The younger brother leaves from there in despair. Another man was watching all this. That man starts following him. The younger brother reaches the rented house. He sees. Father and other brothers were fast asleep on the bed. The door was open. Suddenly that man comes in the room and starts threatening the younger brother. He starts saying - Leave the investigation and inquiry of that murder, otherwise I will kill you. Hearing this, the younger brother gets scared and says. Okay, okay. That man leaves from there. After that he takes a deep breath, wipes the sweat from his forehead. Closes the door and sleeps on the bed with his other brothers. Third day. There is a knock on the door. The younger brother opens the door. There was a crowd of students outside. The students were accusing the younger brother that he is the culprit, he is the culprit. Because the second day, he was searching for something at that place. The police officer, after hearing all this, does not arrest him because his picture was not in the CCTV footage installed at the college gate. The police officer knew that the culprit was someone from the college itself. But who? The police officers did not know this yet. Nor was the knife found. On the fourth day. Father and three brothers sit in the vehicle and start going towards home. But the younger brother and his uncle's elder brother get down to buy some stuff. After buying stuff, they run towards the vehicle, but the vehicle misses. There is a sound of a collision. When they look, they see that a woman has met with an accident with her scooty. They pick up that woman and make her lie down at a place. After that they call the ambulance. The ambulance arrives after about half an hour. The ambulance takes that woman to the hospital. Both of them stand on the side of the road and start waiting for another vehicle. The second vehicle comes and stops. First the uncle's elder son gets on the vehicle and comes back after some time. There was a different happiness on his face. The vehicle was stopped there. What is inside the vehicle? The younger brother also goes inside the vehicle to see it. The younger brother is surprised to see this scene. A foreign woman was sitting completely naked on a soft bed inside the vehicle. That woman was smiling looking at him. The younger brother could not resist. He also became completely naked and started having vaginal sex with her for a long time. Then a voice comes - get up! It has been a long time. He wakes up from sleep. He realizes that it was just a dream. He starts looking here and there and starts thinking about the dream he saw in sleep. His eyes fall on his pants. Which had become a little wet. After that he gets up from the bed and goes to wash his hands and face.

The Tragedy - Today Adolf killed two rats by drowning them in water. Some day, he poured oil on the stairs and made one of his family members fall. Sometimes he threw the dog from the roof. Every day he tortured and killed some animal or the other. He enjoyed doing all this. The family members were worried. Adolf was almost 18 years old. It was four o'clock in the night. Adolf wore his slippers and came out of the house. He was walking on the dirt road. He saw a heap of sand. He went near the heap and started playing with the sand. There was a huge mango tree there. Sounds started coming from the branches of the tree. Adolf looked up. His forehead started getting covered with sweat. A black monkey was looking at him angrily. Its eyes had turned red. A few days ago,

Adolf had set fire to that monkey on the pretext of giving it food. That monkey saved its life by going to the nearby pond. But his body had turned black. Adolf got up from there and started running. Someone had left an axe there. The monkey jumped from the tree and started running towards Adolf with the axe. Adolf's foot hit a stone. He fell down. He was about to attack him with the axe when Adolf wakes up from sleep screaming loudly. He looks around. He realizes that it was just a dream. He goes to the place where he had brutally burnt the monkey. Seeing the dead body of the monkey, he laughs loudly. Then a thick trunk of a mango tree breaks and falls on him. He gets injured and gets buried under it. He lies lifeless for several hours. After that, his family members come and admit him to the hospital. After suffering from pain for several days. After getting treatment. After about a few months, he gets well. The family members explain again - don't do wrong things. Hearing this Adolf starts laughing. Angry, his mother slaps him. Some days pass. It was evening time. Adolf was looking here and there from the roof. A tap was being made at some distance. His eyes fell on his father. Who was helping in making the tap. He came down the stairs. While walking he started moving towards his father. The sun was setting. The work of the tap was completed. His father started going through the short-cut path. Which was a kutcha path. Adolf started following him. The distance between them was around 10 meters. His father turned from the path and started moving towards the house. Adolf was also about to turn and move towards the house when a woman held his hand tightly. There were two more men with that woman. He thought, these people were not kidnappers. At that time Adolf was so scared that he was not able to speak. He was trying hard to free his hand. All three of them were laughing in a scary way. Adolf bit their hand with his teeth and ran towards his house after freeing his hand. Two weeks later. Adolf along with his companions plan to rob a small bank. Then a baby goat starts licking his feet. Adolf gets angry and kicks it hard. After which it starts crying loudly. Seeing this, Adolf becomes very happy in his heart. His companions feel bad about this behavior of Adolf. Night time. They wear black clothes and try to break the lock of the bank at around four in the night. Due to the loud noise, after some time police officers reach there. They start running from there. The officers fire bullets. But the bullets go past them. They keep running for a long time. They reach inside a small forest. After some time it is morning. They look at the top of a tree. Their hearts start beating fast due to fear. A man was hanging from a noose on top of a tree. Seeing this scene, they run towards their house at a fast pace. It was around 11 o'clock at night. It was a moonlit night. Adolf opens the door and looks down the stairs. There a clown was looking at Adolf with a scary smile. Adolf, scared, slams the door shut. His elder brother asks him - what happened? He says - nothing. In the evening. He was going on the road. He finds a revolver lying there. He picks it up and keeps it with him. He starts moving forward. Ahead of him, a wedding procession was going. In that procession, a clown was dancing slowly. Adolf fires a bullet at the clown with his revolver. After being hit by the bullet, the clown falls down on the ground. Adolf runs away from there. After a few hours, he realises that it was another clown. But instead of feeling remorse, he laughs out loud. He takes his revolver and starts shooting at the animals that come near him. Five innocent animals are shot dead on the spot. The next day, an investigation begins into the incident. But he goes to another city. To a relative's wedding. The wedding preparations were going on. A girl takes him by the hand and takes him up the stairs to a room. There was a 'Khant' (a wooden stool) kept there. Adolf thinks - she probably wants to have sex with me. Adolf climbs on top of her. Excited, he ejaculates in his pants. The girl's mother and Adolf's father were already present in the room. They were hiding. When Adolf sees his father, he stands up in fear. His father gets angry and leaves without saying anything. The girl and her mother also leave. Adolf, a little sad, starts coming down the stairs. He starts walking in a field situated some distance away from the wedding house. Something is visible in the moonlight. He felt that there was something under his feet. But what was it? He did not know. He looks ahead. In front of the wedding house, a tree had been lit up. Under it, a baby goat was smiling at Adolf. Adolf thinks a lot. After that, he realizes that it is an old landmine. He drowns in sorrow for some time. He regrets remembering his bad deeds. After that, he smiles at the baby goat and moves his foot away. There is an explosion and his body is blown to pieces.

Uncontrolled Helicopter - Siddu was a strong nineteen-year-old boy. His body was a little bulky and fat. Other boys used to make fun of him. They used to tease him by calling him elephant. Also, no one used to play with him or go out with him. He used to feel sad. One day he went to a fair. He parked his bicycle and started watching cricket. Some boys of his village were playing cricket at some distance from the fair. In a rough field. He was sitting alone at one place. A ball comes to him. A mischievous boy named Chitman. He comes to Siddu, abuses his mother and says- Give the ball here. Siddu gets angry and throws the ball towards the bushes with force using his hand. After that all the boys present there come and tell Siddu- If you do not find the ball, then tomorrow we all will beat you. They leave from there. Siddu alone starts searching for the ball in the bushes. After some time, it was about to be evening. He does not find the ball. Disappointed, he takes his bicycle and goes home. The next day. Siddu's father had bought a new ball a few weeks ago. He gives his new ball to those boys. They become happy after getting the new ball. But Chitman did not enjoy it much. Because Chitman had come here to enjoy beating Siddu. But something else happened. Still Chitman calls him a big fool and goes away from there. Siddu used to feed biscuits to the sheep and goats sometimes. He used to get a lot of happiness by doing this. It was evening time. He wore his slippers and started going towards the garden. There two girls started calling him. He reached the girls. The girls said - Will you help us? He said - What kind of help? The girls said - Will you help us in checking the condom. Siddu hesitated a bit and said - Yes, of course. Siddu started having sex with those girls wearing different condoms. Siddu was enjoying it a lot. He had sex for the first time. The sun had set. It was dark and there was no one around. After completing this task, Siddu and those girls went to their respective homes. After using the mobile for a long time, Siddu lay down on the roof, spreading a blanket to sleep. Then an uncontrolled helicopter is seen flying a few meters above the roof. A man wearing a yellow jersey was seen sitting on the back seat of the helicopter. Siddu felt that the helicopter might fall on him. The uncontrolled helicopter kept flying here and there and fell on the wall in the courtyard of Chitman's house. What happened? To see this, Siddu got up in a hurry and started looking from the roof. He prayed to God and started thinking in his mind. If this uncontrolled helicopter had fallen on me, what a big accident could have happened. Due to the fall of the uncontrolled helicopter, the wall had broken and fallen down. More and more people were gathering there. Flames started coming out of the helicopter. A lot of smoke was coming out and rising towards the sky.

A Young Woman - Mindani was very beautiful. When she was born, her parents died in an accident. She was brought up by her grandmother. She used to blog from a young age. In which her grandmother used to support her a lot. She left her studies after tenth class. After a few years, her YouTube channel had become very famous. Now she had also started earning online. Now she used to travel to new places with her grandmother. She used to create new blogs. She used to get a lot of views and likes. After a few days, Mindani goes to the market to buy vegetables. A young man named Sonich. Who was a drug addict. He used to harass some girl every day. He comes to her and says:- Will you have sex with me. At first, Mindani is surprised to hear this. After that, she gets angry and says no to him. Sonich used to watch porn videos and take drugs every day. Due to Sonich's bad habits, his father left him and settled in another city. His mother had already passed away. He used to work as a clown in a circus. That was his livelihood. It was night time. Mindani's grandmother was fast asleep. It was 1 o'clock in the night. Her grandmother was fast asleep. Mindani was unable to sleep. So she was watching reels on her smartphone. There was silence all around. She started hearing loud noises from the door of the house. When she looked through the window, she got scared. Sonich, dressed as a clown, was banging the door loudly. He had an axe in his hand. Sonich sees Mindani. He looks at her with a scary smile. After that, he starts hitting the wooden door with the axe. Mindani's face fills with fear. Without delay, she calls 100. The police station was about a kilometer away from here. So the policemen reach here very soon. The door was broken. Sonich was about to enter the house when the policemen caught him. Mindani feels relieved. Even now the grandmother was fast asleep. In the morning. She tells the whole incident to the grandmother. Hearing this, the grandmother gets very scared. After this incident, Mindani donates 25 percent of her earnings to orphanages. She also helps the needy. By doing this, she feels a different kind of happiness. One month later. Mindani and her grandmother go for a walk in the forest. The grandmother told her many times:- We should not stay here at night. How could the grandmother leave her alone? Both of them made a tent and spent the night. Necessary things were present in the tent. Three days ago. Sonich got released from jail by giving a bribe of twenty five thousand to a policeman. Immediately after his release, he started searching for Mindani. Now Mindani was listening to stories with her head on Dadi's lap. Both of them were unaware that Sonich was present in the forest. The moon was shining in the moonlit night. Some things were visible in its light. Sonich suddenly enters the tent and drags Mindani out. She screams loudly. Sonich hits her on the head with a stick. Due to which she gets injured. He attacks her to satisfy his lust. But Dadi hits him on the head with a stick and injures him. Dadi picks up Mindani and says:- Daughter, run away from here. I will take care of her. Mindani starts running away from there, falling down. Then Sonich gets angry and ties Dadi's neck with the rope tied to the tent and starts pulling the other end to the tree. Dadi starts suffocating. He hangs Dadi with a noose and ties the other end to the tree. Grandma writhes in pain for some time. After that she dies. Now Sonich starts following her. Mindani reaches near a high waterfall. Mindani pushes a stone into the waterfall and hides somewhere. Sonich comes there. He heard the sound of someone falling into the waterfall. He goes near the waterfall and looks. He feels that the girl has jumped into the waterfall. He was regretting not being able to satisfy his lust. He thought. At least I will find another girl. He moves his feet to go from there. Then his foot slips and his head hits a stone hard. He falls from a height into the waterfall. After writhing in pain for some time. He dies a painful death. His dead body was floating in the fast flowing water. Mindani comes near the tent. Seeing Grandma hanging from the tree, she faints and falls down. In the morning. The forest officer comes there and brings her grandmother down and sprinkles water on Mindani, bringing her back to consciousness. She is taken to the hospital. After a few days, the bribe-taking policeman is removed from his post. The grandmother's body is buried in the ground. Now Mindani sells that house and starts living in an orphanage, spending time with the children.

Third Person - Remu, the elder son of the parents, had developed a habit of addiction. Most of the time he was busy in gambling online and consuming drugs. His parents scolded him many times. But he would not listen to them. Nor would he pay attention to what the family members said. The parents thought - why not get the elder son married. Maybe with the arrival of a daughter-in-law, he will improve. They started looking for a match for him. After looking at many girls. Finally he liked a girl. After a few months. They got married. Both of them were happy. After a few days. Remu's wife - Vasuna. Goes to her maternal home. Remu was unaware that a third person had already entered between them. Vasuna had fallen in love with her real uncle's son Siduram. Vasuna and Siduram had started loving each other since childhood. When Vasuna passed the tenth grade examination. The talk of her marriage started in the family. Due to which Siduram once found Vasuna alone, applied sindoor on her maang and ran away from there. Now Vasuna's post-wedding rituals were being completed at her maternal home. As soon as Siduram saw Vasuna, he kept looking at her. His eyes were not moving away from her. He was just looking at her. Remu left his wife at her maternal home and went to his home the very next day. When all the rituals were completed, Vasuna was sitting alone in the room, enhancing her makeup. Then Siduram comes in the room. Vasuna and Siduram look at each other for some time. After that he comes and sits next to Vasuna. Both talk for a long time. After that they both have sex. After a month. Remu brings her back to her in-laws. Vasuna goes to her maternal home on every festival. This sequence of Siduram and Vasuna continued. After Remu and Vasuna's relationship for many months. After about eight months, Vasuna gives birth to a child. Who is named Taruni. After a few months, the mother-in-law and daughter-in-law start quarreling. The daughter-in-law also leaves the household work, puts the child to sleep or hands over the child to her father-in-law, and spends most of the time watching TV. When she feels like it, she does a little work. She talks to Siduram on the phone in such an excited manner that Remu starts suspecting her. Due to which Remu scolds her many times, pretending to be her second sister. But it does not have much effect on her. Remu was still looking for work. His wife now insists on going to her parents' house every two or one and a half months. Due to which Remu gets angry many times. After a year, Vasuna divorces Remu and after abusing him, fighting with him, she takes her daughter with her to Siduram. Remu stands there sadly and watches. After that, Remu and his family also come to know about this. Siduram was also an unemployed youth. His father used to sell smartphones. She tells Siduram- Now we can get married. Siduram says- I cannot marry you. Siduram leaves from there. In reality Siduram did not love Vasuna. He was just pretending and satisfying his lust. At that time Vasuna started regretting a lot. She sat down on her knees. Slow rain started falling. Tears started falling from Vasuna's eyes. Her parents also did not allow Vasuna to stay in the house. A few weeks after this incident, Remu went out to work. Three years later. Seduram had opened a shop by taking a loan from the bank. But it did not work and he drowned in debt. Remu now works in a company on a good salary. On the other hand, Vasuna lives in a rented house and feeds herself and her daughter by doing sewing work. Sometimes Remu comes to meet his daughter. I would buy the things she needed and show her love.

Chandralekha - In the 16th century. The king of a small kingdom was Chandrasej. The name of his kingdom was Satnampur. The kingdom of Satnampur was flourishing. Chandrasej had an only daughter. Whose name was Chandralekha. She was about 20 years old. She was an expert in dancing. She was also very beautiful. Her dance and beauty were discussed all over the kingdom. Chandrasej and his wife were very worried about her marriage. They were always afraid that some other powerful king might attack our kingdom. A few years later. It was the day of Diwali. The whole kingdom was shining with the light of diyas. The festival was being celebrated with great pomp. A spy comes panting and says- A ruthless king Nagavannam is moving towards our kingdom with his huge army. He is so ruthless that after conquering the kingdom. He kidnaps all the women present in the kingdom and burns the rest alive. Hearing this, the happiness and joy of the people of the kingdom vanishes in a few moments. It is also said about him that a year ago, he killed his father and became the king himself. Chandrasej had enough time to go far away with his family. But when he saw the sad and scared faces of the people of the kingdom, he decided to fight. Chandrasej said to his daughter - Chandralekha, you take your mother and go far away from here on a fast horse. But his daughter refuses to run away from here and decides to fight. Many people of the kingdom start fleeing from here. At the same time, many people of the kingdom are ready to support the king. After some time, a series of screams and shouts start in the kingdom. The war had started on the dark night of Amavasya. Soldiers were fighting from both sides. On the other hand, Chandralekha had also taken up the sword in her hand. She was somehow fighting the soldiers with her sword in the light of torches. Nagavannam's eyes fall on Chandralekha. He gets mesmerized by her beauty. The soldiers are ordered that no soldier will make any lethal attack on that girl. After a few hours, King Chandrasej loses this war. King Nagavannam gives orders to his soldiers in front of Chandralekha. After that, Nagavannam's soldiers, along with her father, pour kerosene on the remaining soldiers, people and children and burn them alive. The whole Satnampur reverberates with screams. Tears start falling from Chandralekha's eyes. After a few minutes, everything becomes quiet in this dark night. Nagavannam and his soldiers kidnap the women of the kingdom. For many days, his soldiers forcefully quench their thirst with those women. Nagavannam had heard a lot about Chandralekha's dance. But I had never seen her dance with my own eyes. King Nagavannam had forced her to dance many times. But she did not listen. Every night, Nagavannam would force Chandralekha to satisfy his lust. Also, if she did not listen, he would beat her body with a whip. Wounds had appeared on her body. Chandralekha had stopped eating and drinking. Day by day, her body was getting weaker. She thought to herself. If only she had listened to her father that day, then perhaps she would not have to see this day. It was midnight. King Nagavannam, after having his meal, went towards Chandralekha's room. When he opened the door, he saw that Chandralekha was hanging from a noose. After that. King Nagavannam started to remain drunk and worried most of the time. After a few months. When the king did not come out of his room for two days, the ministers broke the door and went inside. They saw that King Nagavannam was sitting lifelessly on a chair. When the doctor comes and examines them, it is found that they had died of a heart attack two days ago. After the death of the king, a rebellion begins in that kingdom. In which the commander and many soldiers are killed. After a few weeks, this rebellion calms down. Later it is found out that Nagavannam's younger sister

Nagendi was behind this rebellion. The commander himself wanted to become the king. That is why Nagendi planned this rebellion. Nagendi becomes the queen of that kingdom and starts ruling. Chandralekha's mother fainted in the battlefield. Due to which the soldiers thought that she had died and they left from there. People hiding far away treated her mother and saved her life. When the news of the death of her husband and daughter reaches her, she drowns in a bottomless ocean of sorrow. But after a few days, Chandralekha's mother says in anger - Just as he has destroyed my family, in the same way I will extinguish even the last lamp of his family. The painful death of her husband and daughter had made her ruthless. Six months later. Chandralekha's mother Hemvati reaches Nagendi's kingdom. After a lot of effort, Hemvati gets a job as a maid in her palace. Queen Nagendi had a son who was only seven years old. Due to Hemvati's concentration towards work, Queen Nagendi also used to praise her many times. In just a month, she had become quite friendly with everyone. It was evening time. The queen's son was playing on the roof of the palace. There were dark clouds in the sky. It was about to rain. So Hemvati was taking down the clothes from the ropes. Hemvati's eyes fall on the queen's son. She throws the clothes on the ground and forcefully picks up the queen's son and throws him down from the roof. There is a loud thud. The queen looks towards the roof. Hemvati also jumps down with a scary smile. Due to falling from a height, Hemvati dies on the spot. The queen runs to her son and picks him up in her arms. There was a lot of blood flowing from his head. But fate had something else in store for him. His breathing was slow. But both his legs were broken. Without any delay, he was taken to a senior officer. After three years of treatment, he recovered. But his legs were no longer alive. Now he could never walk on his feet. Also, there was a possibility of brain injury sometimes. Her son was now ten years old. The people of Satnampur state get this news. After that, he was attacked many times. Now the queen was very scared about her son. She gives her palace to a trust for orphans and goes abroad with her son. It is said that after that, Queen Nagendi never returned to her kingdom.